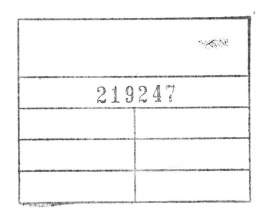

LOVE IN THE AFTERNOON
AND OTHER DELIGHTS

LOVE IN THE AFTERNOON

And Other Delights

Penny Vincenzi

WINDSOR
PARAGON

First published 2013
by Headline Review
This Large Print edition published 2013
by AudioGO Ltd
by arrangement with
Headline Publishing Group

Hardcover   ISBN: 978 1 4713 5472 4
Softcover   ISBN: 978 1 4713 5473 1

British Library Cataloguing in Publication Data available

Printed and bound in Great Britain by
TJ International Ltd

For Daughters One, Two, Three and Four.
With much love.

CONTENTS

INTRODUCTION

It's really rather nice to be publishing my short stories all in one piece; I've written them pretty sporadically over the years, when I'm asked by sundry magazines and newspapers. I read them when they come out, file them away (which means putting them in an enormous cardboard box in my study labelled 'Short Stories') and forget about them. So not a particularly tidy process.

And here they are, neatly got together, bringing back (in some cases quite vividly) the occasion or time that inspired them: a particular Mother's Day, perhaps, or a Christmas party, or a visit to New York.

'The Glimpses' was the first fiction I ever wrote, and it was a bit like discovering you can ride a bicycle: a few bumps and scrapes, a lot of falls and thinking you'll never manage it, and then suddenly, oh my goodness, you're flying along and you can't quite believe it. So that is my special favourite.

'The Brooch' was inspired by a real brooch, exactly as described in the story, which sat on my grandmother's rather ample bosom while she read to me. I loved and wanted that brooch so much, but of course was never allowed even to hold it. It was part of my childhood, and it seemed to me something that deserved a story of its own.

'Baby Knows Best' was sparked off by my own experiences as a mother and grandmother, discovering over and over again that babies have a mind of their own and there is very little you can do about it.

'The Best Table' started out as a true story, with a trip to New York and the Hamptons, and a chance meeting with a very charming chap on the Hampton Jitney, the bus that goes out from Manhattan on Saturday mornings, bearing lots of rich, well-dressed weekenders. I suddenly felt I was living out a romantic comedy which deserved a better twist than the real-life one, which wasn't a twist at all, just a nice weekend.

And so on.

The thing about writing short stories is that they do need a twist, and a neat one at that. You can't just ramble on; there has to be a beginning, and a middle, and then quite a swift end, which must surprise and intrigue. So just because they're short doesn't mean they're easy to write; rather the reverse. But I do love doing them—occasionally— as they require a rather different approach. Normally I don't have the faintest idea what's going to happen at the end of my books, or even halfway through; I simply follow my characters and see what they get up to. That's a bit of an understatement, and makes it sound quite a lot easier than it is, but it is nonetheless true.

With a short story, I really do know what's going to happen, no room for surprises. It's not how I like to write all the time—I'd find it quite boring—but occasionally—well, it's a bit like having a difficult workout at the gym: I feel challenged and rather pleased with myself when I've managed it.

As for the articles, well, I'm still really a journalist at heart. If somebody woke me up at two in the morning and asked me before I was properly awake what I did for a living, I'd probably say journalist, rather than novelist. Newspaper ink runs in my veins, as they say. When I reread my piece about Marjorie Proops, the famous agony aunt, once my boss at the *Daily Mirror*, I find myself right back there, sitting in that noisy newsroom, thick with cigarette smoke as it was then, and the incredible clatter of typewriters.

Journalism still seems to me the best job in the world, and amazingly privileged: you can meet people you'd never meet in the normal course of events, anyone you put your mind to really; go to places you'd never go, see things you'd never see.

It's also very nice the way I do it now, sitting peacefully at home, thinking on the page, rather than having to write a thousand words in half an hour, with a subeditor standing over me, his hand literally held out for the paper as it emerges from the typewriter. It's extremely self-indulgent this way, penning opinions, as in the piece about being a mother, dragging humour out of situations, as in my experiences of 'Getting Older', or simply answering questions about my favourite books. Not really proper journalism at all, I suppose, but always nice to be asked to do it, and to have it done and dusted in half a day rather than the two years each book takes.

It's all writing, of course, but it's all very different. Being able to write fiction doesn't mean you can write articles about people, for instance. But it's a bit like playing the piano and the violin: doing one doesn't mean you can go straight into the other if you've never done it before, but you're off to a head start. You can read music, and you know what a note should sound like; the rest is practice.

I do hope you're going to enjoy the results here of an awful lot of practice!

3

Short Stories

LOVE IN THE AFTERNOON

All her friends thought it was wonderful that Anna visited her grandfather in the nursing home every other Sunday; Anna didn't think it was wonderful at all. She loved old people, always had done; she enjoyed chatting—or rather listening—to them, hearing their life stories, borne back through time, half, perhaps three quarters of a century. It was partly, she knew, because she loved stories, filing them away in her mind, occasionally noting down a few details in the leather-bound notebook her grandfather had given her for that very purpose.

Which was why she was here today. She had brought it in a few weeks ago, to show him how battered and well used it was, only to find that he had become ill, and was being admitted to hospital for tests. In the panic, she had left it behind.

He had never come back from the hospital. Anna's mother had collected all his things, but not the notebook.

'I don't know where it is, darling, I'm sorry. Maybe Matron will know.'

Matron did know. 'Your grandfather's girlfriend was entrusted with it,' she said. 'Mrs Lesley, you know?'

Anna did know. Rose Lesley was fairly new to the nursing home, a pretty, rather grand old lady, with snow-white hair and brilliant blue eyes. Her grandfather had been very taken with her.

'If you could bear to come in,' Matron said, 'I know Mrs Lesley would love to see you. She misses your grandfather dreadfully.'

7

Anna said she would, and the next Sunday afternoon she drove her mother's Mini over to Helena House.

Rose was in the garden, sitting under the big chestnut tree. 'Your grandfather was so proud of you,' she said, patting the seat beside her, 'and so sure you'd achieve your ambition of becoming a writer. And having had a look at some of your ideas—I hope you don't mind, my dear—I'm sure he was right.'

'Well, I hope so,' said Anna. 'I haven't even got to university yet. I'm still waiting for my A-level results.'

'What's that got to do with it?' said Rose. 'Writing stories is a gift, not something you learn. Do you think Shakespeare did his A levels, or Chaucer?'

Anna said she thought probably not.

'I miss your grandfather,' said Rose sadly. 'Very much. He was such a gentleman; he had style. Not many of the people here have style.'

Anna had to admit this was true.

'Style is terribly important,' Rose said. 'It tells you a lot about people. My mother had great style.' After a pause she added, 'Even after my father died and left us—her—penniless, she always looked wonderful.'

Anna sat silent, feeling a story coming her way.

'Dudley, my first husband, was very stylish also,' Rose said. 'We were a most dashing couple. And of course the thirties were a very glamorous time. Goodness, we had fun. Oh, but you don't want to hear about that . . .'

Anna said she did, as Rose had known she would, and for the rest of the afternoon they

8

drifted into the magical world of Rose's youth: of fine London houses and country weekends, of dazzling parties and smart nightclubs, of trips to Le Touquet in private planes . . . 'And the women were so elegant—those bias-cut crêpe dresses and marcel-waved hair. And oh—the fur coats I had! Two or three, and the most wonderful collection of cigarette holders. One had real diamonds in it, from Asprey, a present from an admirer.'

'He must have admired you very much,' Anna said, 'to give you that.'

'Well, darling, of course he did. He became my lover. He gave me a pair of slave bangles too, gold set with emeralds, very beautiful. He was an Indian prince,' she added, with a touch of complacency.

'And did—did your husband know about this?' asked Anna, given courage by Rose's frankness.

'Oh, I think so. We never discussed it—you didn't then; there was none of this soul-baring. Marriage was a business and you ran it well, and if love faded a little, that didn't mean life couldn't be very pleasant. I ran my marriage extremely well,' she added. 'Dudley often said what a wonderful wife I was. And then the war came, and he went into the army, left me on the morning of the ninth of June 1940, sent to Italy, and I never saw him again.'

She lay back in the seat and closed her eyes. 'Darling, I'm terribly tired. I can't talk any more now. Will you come back? Another afternoon? My daughters come in the mornings—you wouldn't want to waste time with them. My son is more interesting: he lives in California, works in the film industry.'

And so the afternoons of love, as Anna thought of them, began. She visited Rose every Sunday, and looked forward to it all week. It was like watching some wonderful film or TV series.

The war led to many love affairs: 'Life was so tenuous, darling, you might never see someone again, so of course you wanted to be happy with them. And to help them forget what they were going back to. London was wonderful then, in spite of the danger. We used to go to the Dorchester in big parties, drink cocktails and eat wonderful dinners and then dance almost all night.'

'What about air raids?'

'Oh, we used to go down to the Turkish baths in the basement—perfectly safe—clutching our drinks; it was rather fun. You had to pay extra for your dinner, a few shillings, but then you could have anything you wanted: smoked salmon, asparagus . . .' Her voice tailed off.

The great love of Rose's wartime years had been a 'wonderfully handsome' pilot who had covered himself in glory during the Battle of Britain and then been killed in an air raid on his first night of leave in London. 'I wanted to die too, it hurt so much—we were setting off on a little holiday the next day from my house in Chelsea; I waited for hours and hours, and he'd never been late, so I think I knew. Afterwards, I discovered he was going to propose—his best friend told me and said he'd shown him the ring.'

She had worked in a Red Cross canteen several nights a week, had a brief fling with a naval commander and another with a 'divine major'—and we think we have sexual freedom, thought Anna— but came to the end of the war 'a little tired and actually rather broke'.

'I thought then I'd had enough of love, that I

10

wanted security and friendship. I was so lucky I met Richard. Richard was quite—quite plain, darling, a little sturdy, but so sweet and gentle and oh, he adored me. And he was pretty well off. We got married all at once and I made my vows that day knowing my romancing was over. Only it wasn't, of course.'

She had a talent for storytelling, knew exactly how to bring a time alive, when to end an episode. As the summer wore on, Anna finished her holiday job and started to visit Rose twice, three times a week.

'So sweet of you, darling, to listen to my nonsense,' Rose would say, and Anna would smile and say she never wanted it to end.

Rose was thirty-five when she married Richard. 'It was such a dreary time, just after the war; everything was still rationed and there was no fun, no sense of adventure to get you through it. We lived in Kent, in a rather nice house, and Richard went to the City every day. I was a little bored, but I was determined to be a good wife, and I looked after him very well. The girls were born, and Richard was so happy, a wonderful father. It was a magnificent era for the theatre—*Oklahoma!*, *Annie Get Your Gun*—and we'd take a few friends, stay up in town, at the Savoy usually, but it wasn't nearly so romantic as in the war. And then—well, then I met the love of my life . . .'

Anna recognised the cue for the interval and left.

*   *   *

Next afternoon, when she arrived at Helena House, Rose had a bad cold. 'So don't stay too long and

11

make her tired,' Matron said. Anna promised.

And then the most romantic chapter of Rose's life began.

'I was a little bit down, getting bored with country life—I missed all my London friends terribly. And then—oh darling, then I met Jonathan. At a cocktail party. My knees went weak. He was absolutely the most beautiful man I had ever seen; he was an artist, and he wore the most marvellous clothes: jeans—which hardly anyone wore then—and white shirts, always white shirts, open at the neck, and beautiful velvet smoking jackets. But none of that mattered, you know; I should have loved him if he'd had one eye and been totally bald.'

Anna thought this probably unlikely, but she smiled at Rose and poured her another cup of tea.

'He was quite shy, in spite of his looks; not a smooth operator at all. That was what I loved most. He had a slight stammer, too, and it just turned my heart over.

'Anyway, I tried to resist, both of us did, but it was absolutely overwhelming. I knew it was so bad of me, but Richard had no idea. I used to go up and see Jonathan twice a week in his studio. I lived for these afternoons, alone with him. His studio was in Chelsea, by the river Thames, and I can still see the reflection of the river on the ceiling. We would sit on the little balcony, drinking some rather beastly red wine, trying to decide what to do. It wasn't just an affair, you see—we wanted to be together for ever.

'When I was with him I wanted to stay, but the minute I left and was on the train again, going home, the torture began. I would think 'I couldn't

12

leave Richard; he would be a completely broken man. He was quite proud and stuffy, you see—how could he explain to the world that his wife had left him for an artist . . .?'

Her voice had tailed off; she was asleep.

Two afternoons later, when Anna returned, Matron was in Rose's room. She shook her head and said, very quietly, 'Not today, Anna, she's too tired.'

'Nonsense,' came the voice from the bed, 'I'm not tired at all. And Anna and I have important things to talk about.'

Matron withdrew with a warning look at Anna.

'Give me your hand, darling. I so love our afternoons. And I have so much to tell you today.' But the hand was very warm and the cheeks were flushed. She talked faster than usual.

'So, darling, there I was, trapped. It was love or duty, and I was never very good at duty. And I loved Jonathan so much. He was the first thing I thought of in the morning and the last thing at night; he made the sun shine for me, on the rainiest day. The prospect of life without him made everything bleak.

'And then I realised I was pregnant. I knew it wasn't Richard's. And Jonathan said that now, of course, I couldn't stay with Richard, I must go to him. I felt I was on the rack. I changed my mind hourly; it was absolutely dreadful. At one point I thought I should leave both of them, go away on my own. But then there would have been three of us unhappy. Oh dear . . .' Two large tears rolled down her flushed face; she was reliving her unhappiness.

Anna stood up. 'Dear Rose, you must stop now, you're so tired. I'll come back another day.'

She phoned next day. Matron said Rose was very

13

unwell. 'Bronchitis, possibly pneumonia.'

It became pneumonia.

*   *   *

Anna went to say goodbye to Rose. Her breathing was very fast, very shallow. She was wearing an oxygen mask which she kept pulling off, and was drifting in and out of consciousness. Anna bent and kissed her forehead and stood looking at her for a while, remembering all the stories, all the lovers, wondering if Rose did too.

Rose died that night; Anna stood by the phone, crying at the news, and thought how much she would miss her and how she would never know whether she had indeed chosen love over duty.

She went to the funeral; there were only a few people there. A handful of Rose's friends, the staff of Helena House. Rose's children were in the front pew, two stout, plain women and a tall, grey-haired man with Rose's dazzling smile and brilliant blue eyes. Afterwards, at the nursing home, she introduced herself to them. 'Yes, our mother told us you were visiting her. Most kind,' said one of the women.

'Indeed,' said the other.

'Honestly, I enjoyed it,' said Anna.

'Such a good place, this,' said the first woman. 'Our father was here, you know. In fact, he had the same room.'

'No,' said Anna, 'no, I didn't know that. But I heard a lot about him,' she added, untruthfully. 'He was obviously a wonderful man.'

'He was indeed, wasn't he, girls?' said the man. 'A father in a million. So good to us all. And they

14

were so devoted to one another, until the day he died.'

And in that moment, Anna knew what Rose had decided. She had chosen duty, but she had not entirely lost love. She had stayed with Richard, but she had had Jonathan's baby. A boy, who looked—most fortunately in the circumstances—just like his mother. But who spoke like his father. With a slight stammer.

THE GLIMPSES

James was a very lucky man. He told himself so quite often, and he listened to his mother and his mother-in-law and his wife's best friends (of whom there seemed to be rather a lot) telling him so quite often as well, and he knew he ought to believe it, and in fact he sometimes did. He managed to persuade himself that it was quite true; he would say yes, I am a very lucky man, very lucky indeed, and he would count his blessings again and yet again and congratulate himself upon them.

Since he counted them so extremely frequently, he knew exactly how many there were and the order in which they came: pretty, loving wife; three beautiful children; nice house (in a good area with good schools); good job in insurance, excellent prospects, fair salary; then he was very healthy, he didn't have ulcers, and he could beat someone a fair bit younger than he was at squash; and he and Anne, as the pretty, loving wife was called, had a very active social life and plenty of friends. Yes, he would say, pushing his rose-tinted spectacles more firmly on, yes, I am very lucky, most fortunate, and he would meditate upon his less fortunate friends and relations who had been made redundant or were getting divorced or who did have ulcers, and compare his lot most favourably with theirs.

It wasn't even as if he and Anne had a sterile or even a dull relationship. They talked and discussed a great deal, and even after nine years they were lovers as well as friends, as she liked to say, and in fact said quite often, and it was true, of course. Every six days or so, Anne would turn the light out before he had finished reading, unbutton her Laura Ashley nightie and say 'James' in a particular tone of voice that was an interesting hybrid of question and command. She always assumed he would be ready for her, and of course he usually was, although there were times when he could have wished either for a variation in her approach or more sympathy with his own mood.

Anne had done a course in self-awareness at the Adult Education Centre, and she knew that it was most important that women should take the initiative in sex whenever they so wished. Moreover, she was aware that a woman had particular desires and needs of her own, as well as recognising those of her man; and although she didn't actually feel those needs very strongly herself, she nevertheless wanted James to recognise their existence and how important they were, and not to regard their sex life as simply a gratification of his own.

James knew, from listening to the coarse banter of his colleagues and squash opponents in various pubs and bars, that they would regard this attitude of Anne's as still further manifestation of his great good fortune, for many of them had to work quite

16

hard to be allowed to gratify their desires, and they would have given their next promotion or place on the squash ladder in exchange for a wife who issued sexual invitations on a regular basis, however predictable they might be. And it wasn't even totally predictable really, James supposed: Anne was quite enthusiastic, just unimaginative, and afterwards, when she had climbed back into her Laura Ashley nightie and was talking about her day, which was what she liked to do, he would stroke her hair tenderly and reflect on his fondness for her, and wrench his thoughts away from the disorder of desire and the flesh and back into the neat lines of the PTA, the babysitting rota, the children's progress with their reading and recorder playing, and the literary luncheon appreciation group which Anne had formed.

There he was then, very lucky, very lucky indeed. So how was it, he wondered, that so often, indeed with appalling frequency, depression would strike him in the stomach like a physical blow, the rose-tinteds would slither right to the end of his nose and fall off, and he would see his life for what it really was? And what it really was he knew he didn't really want. What he did want was slightly out of focus and very much out of reach; but he also knew that it was the real thing, not a fantasy, and that if it ever did come along, he would recognise it and reach out for it without hesitation.

It shimmered tantalisingly, both in his subconscious and in the real world, but occasionally he would catch a fleeting glimpse of it, and it was like suddenly recognising the beloved only just ahead, yet out of reach, and his heart would thud, his knees jellify, and he would reach forward, trying

17

desperately to catch hold of it, to detain it before it was lost once more in the crowd.

The Glimpses, the fleeting glances, sometimes took the form of people, but more often they were an environment, an atmosphere, a feeling of being in the right place at almost the right time. And later, when the Glimpses had gone, and he sat eating Anne's cassoulets and crumbles in the warmth and mess of the family dining room, to the accompaniment of tales of the suburban broods, and much interrupted by small pyjamaed figures, his mind would go back and try to analyse the substance of what he had seen. Gradually the formulation became more precise: what he was glimpsing was beauty, and beauty of a very worldly kind. It was not sunsets or fire glow or the smile on the face of a little child that made him sick with longing (indeed, he had more than enough of all that sort of thing, particularly the smiles on the little faces); it was still white rooms and sculptured furnishings, reedy music and diagrammatic paintings. And the people in the Glimpses were beautiful too: witty and stylish, their conversations designed as carefully as their clothes.

As he began to recognise what he was finding in the Glimpses and why he liked them so much, he was able to look out for them and to see more of them. He took to going to art galleries in his lunch hour, instead of walking in the park; he would wander through smart furniture shops, drinking in the chrome and the marble, so shiny, so perfect, so unsmudged; and as he grew bolder, he would go into the most expensive and chic clothes shops and study not only the cuts and colours on view but the people buying and wearing them, all obviously

18

rich and clever and successful and selfish, not a PTA member nor househusband among them. And although he could not afford the pictures or the clothes or the coffee tables, he would occasionally buy a glass or a handkerchief and he would keep them in his wardrobe, or his desk drawer, as talismans, living proof that there was another world somewhere, whose lifeblood was not Ribena and finger paints, but fine wine and beautiful books, and the air of which was not filled with action songs and arguments, but esoteric melodies and abstract-based discussions.

Once Anne found a pair of cashmere socks in his wardrobe that he had bought from Paul Smith; her indignation and wrath were more in proportion to the discovery of a batch of lurid love letters. 'Really, James,' she said, hurling them on the bed, 'how could you? They must have cost a fortune. You know Dominic needs new dungarees, and your season ticket's about to expire, and you waste'—she looked at the ticket, quivering with rage—'twenty pounds on a pair of socks. You must be mad, quite, quite mad. Whatever is the matter with you? It's not as if you need socks; I bought you six pairs in Marks in April. I mean, if it was a tie, I could understand a bit more; at least that would show. But socks, why socks?'

Useless to try to explain, James knew. Sitting, head bowed with shame, clutching the socks, symbol of his profligacy and betrayal, he tried to form a coherent sentence about why socks: because they were a luxury, precisely because they didn't show, because they weren't functional, because only he knew that they were there on his feet; expensive, smooth, soft, unstretched from being used as

Christmas stockings. That was why socks.

Later that night, in bed, she was remorseful. 'I'm sorry that I got so cross, darling,' she said. 'Of course if you think you need some socks, then you should buy them. I don't suppose you realised how expensive they were. I'll get you some more tomorrow in Marks, I've got to get Emma some tights, and maybe you could change those for a tie or something.'

'No, it's all right, I really don't need any,' said James with a sigh, turning over and deliberately choosing not to notice that she was unbuttoning her nightie, even though it wasn't scheduled for another two nights at least. 'I'm sorry too, but anyway, I couldn't change them for a tie, that would cost at least thirty-five pounds. Good night.' And as he lay awake in the dark, he drew some shreds of comfort from the fact that he knew exactly how much ties from Paul Smith cost, while Anne hadn't the faintest idea.

After that, he kept all his trophies in the office.

*   *   *

Time passed. The summer holidays (camping in France) came and went, as did Hallowe'en (trick-or-treating with the children) and Guy Fawkes (bonfire in their garden this year, with sausages, tomato soup and mulled wine for all the neighbours), and Christmas began to be heard in the distance.

Anne made endless puddings, cakes and sausage rolls ('for the freezer', she explained, as if it was some kind of huge, hungry animal), sewed for the nativity play and planned carol singing; James worried about paying for it all, wondered whether his mother would actually come to blows with Anne's this year, and received an invitation to a Christmas party at one of the galleries where he had become something of a regular and had actually bought a couple of prints (hanging rather incongruously on his office wall, alongside his charts on pension schemes and his department's annual holiday rota).

He saw the Glimpses swimming suddenly and triumphantly into focus, accepted promptly, and then spent many hours worrying about what to wear; the socks, of course, would be ideal and needed an outing, but something more was needed. Nothing he possessed would be remotely suitable; his smartest suit was outmoded all over by inches, his jeans were over-washed and his casuals only just all right for family Sundays. Finally, feeling rather sick, he took his Barclaycard to Simpsons and bought a light wool beige and brown jacket and some beautifully cut, slightly baggy beige trousers, then, feeling even sicker, a pale blue, faintly patterned silk shirt. It all cost him considerably more than the total allowance he gave Anne to clothe the children for the winter.

Looking at himself in the clothes, though, it was worth the sickening guilt. In the mirror stood not the James he knew—solid, reliable chap, faithful husband, selfless father—but someone else altogether. Smooth, handsome even, possibly unreliable, probably unfaithful and certainly selfish; a person, in fact, from the Glimpses.

He gazed and gazed, enraptured with himself, like an adolescent girl going to a party; then finally, and reluctantly, having taken the clothes off but with some of his new selfishness and style still

21

hung about him, he went to Russell & Bromley and bought a pair of hugely expensive soft leather loafers. He had thought his brogues would possibly do, but they were a sorry piece of sacrilege beneath the trousers, betraying his homely roots; and besides, he felt he owed it to the socks to cover them with class.

Where to keep it all, though? His small pen of an office was clearly unsafe—all he had was a coat hook behind the door—and home was hopeless. Finally, in a flurry of inspiration, he thought of the left-luggage office at Paddington station. He bought a cheap suitcase (totally unworthy of its precious contents, but it couldn't be helped) and deposited the lot. He had not the faintest idea what he could do with them later; he didn't even think about it. He had an appointment with Destiny at the party, he felt, and Destiny could surely take care of a few articles of clothing.

*   *   *

'I'll be late tonight, darling,' he said to Anne at breakfast on the morning of the party. 'Sales department booze-up. Don't worry about me, just go to bed.'

'But Jamie,' said Anne plaintively, 'you know I've got a rehearsal for the carol concert, and Sue can only stay till eight and I told her you'd relieve her then. I know I went through it all with you— Cressida, don't put egg in your pocket. Can't you possibly get out of it, or at least come home early?'

'Sorry, no,' said James, amazed at his own firmness, and fixing his mind firmly on the suitcase at Paddington and its contents to lend him further courage. 'No, I can't. Dominic, stop that at once, I don't want your Ribena. You'll just have to get someone else to babysit for you, Anne, I'm afraid; I'm sorry.'

'But it's not for me, it's for us,' said Anne, looking at him in astonishment at this piece of heresy. 'They're your children as well, not just mine.'

'True,' said James, picking up his briefcase and the paper, 'but it's your carol concert. Bye, darling.'

Anne watched him going down the path and then started clearing up very slowly. He hadn't been the same since she had found the socks.

*   *   *

The clothes were a bit creased when he got them out of the suitcase, but there was nothing he could do about that. He hung them up rather boldly behind his office door and hoped they would look better by six o'clock. They did.

He had his hair cut rather expensively at lunchtime, feeling that at this stage there was no point leaving the icing off the cake—or rather too much on it; he promised Anne mentally as he paid the outrageous bill that he would go without lunch for two months to make up for it.

He waited until most people had gone home, changed in the men's cloakroom, put his work clothes in the suitcase and took it back to the station. Then he took a taxi down to Sloane Street.

He was no longer nervous; he felt, in his new clothes, so different, so absolutely another man, that what he was doing and where he was going seemed entirely right and appropriate, but he

23

did feel an enormous sense of excitement and anticipation, as if he was off to meet some beloved person from whom he had been too long separated.

When he arrived, the party was half complete. James stood in the doorway, holding the glass of champagne he had been handed, simply gazing into the room. Here surely was Elysium, a glittering, glossy paradise: beautiful women, rich men (some of them beautiful too), fine clothes, brittle conversation. He caught snatches of it, as people passed him by: 'Darling . . . such heaven . . . you look marvellous, what have you been doing . . . did you see his last exhibition . . . frightfully overrated . . . Aspen for Christmas . . . new husband . . . absurd divorce case . . . with a wife like that, who needs a mistress . . . absolutely broke . . . sold all his mother's shares . . . tiny house in Nice, do come . . .'

It was like the music of the spheres, and he would have stood there all evening, perfectly content, quite careless of the fact that he could not contribute even a note, had not someone suddenly pushed past him, trodden on his foot and overbalanced, tipping the entire contents of a glass of champagne down his shirt. And then a voice: 'Oh God, how absolutely ghastly, I am so sorry, how could I have done such a stupid thing? Oh, look at your shirt, and it's so beautiful too. What can I do to make amends? Come with me, come on, Jonathan, Jonathan, where are you? Look, it's too awful, look what I've done to this poor man's shirt.'

James felt a hand on his arm, and then saw it sliding down to take his own: a small, white hand, it was, with long red nails, and wearing a selection of fine gold twisty rings. Following the line of the hand up the arm, his eyes took in fine black crêpe (cut away to show much fine white bosom), a mane of streaked blond hair, and a face which could only be described as beautiful, smiling at him encouragingly as its owner pulled him through the crowd.

Now, thought James, if only I could die now, this instant, and I need never see this ending; and afterwards, as he relived the evening a thousand, ten thousand times, he pinpointed that moment as the one he became actually part of the Glimpses, albeit only an associate member.

But he did not die; he found himself alive and rather wet in a small kitchen behind the gallery with the owner of the hand and arm and the bosom and the face dabbing rather helplessly at his shirt and still shouting for Jonathan.

'Where is the silly sod?' she said crossly. 'Talking to some rich Arab, I expect. He's never around when I need him.'

'Er, who is Jonathan?' asked James, thinking he had better at least test his voice and show that he was not actually mute.

'Jonathan, oh, he's my boyfriend,' she said, 'and he owns the gallery. Don't you know him, then? I thought everyone here did.'

'Well no, not really,' said James, and then, terrified lest his credentials weren't going to meet her scrutiny, 'I'm here because I bought a picture once.'

'Oh really, whose?' she asked, recommencing her dabbing. 'Oh dear, this isn't doing any good. Not this creep who's on now, I hope, terrible waste of money. Jonathan, oh there you are, what on earth have you being doing? Look, I've spilt champagne all over this poor man's lovely shirt. What can we do, is it covered by insurance, do you think?'

'I shouldn't think so,' said Jonathan, looking slightly coldly at James and his shirt. 'Awfully sorry about it, of course, but it'll dry-clean OK. You shouldn't have stood anywhere near Georgina, she's hopelessly accident-prone. She's always spilling something over somebody; last time it was best claret over me. At least champagne doesn't show.'

'Oh Jonathan, you are a bastard,' said Georgina, hurling the cloth at him. 'How can you be so unkind, you deserve to be sued. Now look,' she said to James, 'let me at least get you some more champagne. Actually Jonathan is right, champagne doesn't usually stain, but do get it cleaned and send him the bill. It's also true that I am hopelessly accident-prone. You wouldn't believe the things I do: I drove my car over my own bicycle the other night, which didn't do either of them much good. Now look, here's some more champagne. What do you do? I mean, are you a writer or a collector or something terribly glamorous?'

'Er, not exactly,' said James, wondering wildly what he could claim, and settling for the near-truth. 'I'm in . . . well, finance.'

'Oh,' she said, instantly losing interest, 'a bank. I thought you looked a bit different.'

'Well I'm not quite a banker,' said James eagerly and truthfully. 'It's more—well, insurance in a way.'

In every way, he thought, and thought also that he could hardly have said anything more boring. But it seemed not: she brightened up at once. 'Oh,' she said, 'oh, how wonderful. That's amazing; you might be able to help me. Listen, could you possibly, do you think, spare me an hour one day next week to come to my flat? I've just bought a

26

pair of Victorian seascapes, and I'm desperate to get them valued and insured. I think I've been rather clever and they're a bit special, and Jonathan only knows about this sort of tricksy rubbish, he won't even look at them, and the man who usually insures my stuff won't have the faintest idea, he's an absolute philistine. I mean, do you know anything about Victorian paintings at all? It's a new field to me.'

'Well, I do actually,' said James, thinking that there must indeed be a God, and a good one moreover. 'Not a lot, but enough to—well, advise you.'

'Oh, marvellous,' she said, clasping his hand (so that the contents of his glass lapped perilously near the edge). 'Wonderful. So would you, could you, come and have a look at them? Or I could bring them to you, to your office, only they're a bit delicate really, the frames are disintegrating. And I'd probably drop them on the way.'

'Oh no, I'll come to your flat,' said James, trying to sound as if he received such invitations every day. 'Really, I don't mind a bit.'

'You are simply too kind,' said Georgina. 'I couldn't be more grateful. Now look, I'd better go and circulate a bit or Jonathan will sulk all tomorrow, he's so bad-tempered. Have you got a card or anything so I know where to ring? No, look, it's you who's doing the favour, so you ring me, here's my number, whenever it suits you. I'm usually there till twelve, and then I go to my class and then various other places, so it's best to ring early. But really any time will do, I'm sure you're in thousands of desperately high-powered meetings all the time. I do think it's so kind of you.'

27

'No, honestly,' said James, 'it's nothing, really. I'd like to do it.'

'You're sweet,' she said, standing on tiptoe and kissing his cheek. 'I'll wait to hear from you. And I really am so sorry about your shirt. All right, Jonathan, I'm coming . . .'

James left almost at once. He wanted to preserve the perfection of the evening, to put it in some untouchable place in his mind, before it became smudged or even blurred. He walked for hours: up Sloane Street, through the park, down Mount Street and into Bond Street, sitting for some time on one of the seats near Asprey's, gazing at his expensive shoes and remembering with painstaking care every moment of the evening behind him. The Glimpses had been all, more than he had ever dreamt; and he felt not as if he had been in some strange, alien place but rather that he had come safely and at long last home.

*   *   *

And so his new life began. He packed his clothes into the suitcase in the gents at Paddington, replaced the case in the left-luggage office, and then caught the 10.13 home. It seemed astonishing that he could have journeyed so far and so fast, and yet was not even on the last train. Anne was back from choir practice and whirring somewhat aggressively at the sewing machine.

'It's the angels' robes for the playgroup nativity concert,' she said slightly coldly when he asked her what she was doing. 'I told you I had to make them all. Tomorrow I have to start on the haloes. Nobody else was prepared to take them on, and there're

28

only ten days to go. How was the party?'

'Oh, fine,' said James, going quickly into the kitchen. 'You know what these things are like.'

'No, actually, I don't,' said Anne, and no, actually, you don't, thought James, and as with the price of the Paul Smith tie, the thought gave him immense pleasure.

* * *

He telephoned Georgina on Tuesday, rather than Monday, not wishing to appear gauche or even in possession of too much time.

'Hello,' she said, when she answered the phone. 'Yes, who is this?'

'Oh,' said James, 'it's the man from the party.'

'Which party?' she said, sounding puzzled, and he realised that far from the party being the highest pinnacle of her social career, as it had been for him, it was probably one of many identical small mounds.

'Oh, you know,' he said, 'the one at the gallery. You spilt champagne down my shirt.'

'Oh God, yes, how kind of you to ring. You're going to insure my paintings. Wonderful. How's the shirt?'

'Oh, it's fine,' said James, thinking of it rather sadly as it lay, uncared for and slightly smelly, in the suitcase. 'Really, no damage.'

'Oh good,' said Georgina. 'Jonathan was right— he usually is, it's such a drag. Now, when can you come round?'

'Well, how's tomorrow?' asked James.

'Perfect,' she said. 'Come about eleven, and then I'll buy you lunch afterwards, to say thank you.'

'Oh no, you mustn't,' said James, horrified at the thought of more appalling sartorial shortfall. He could just about, he thought, get away with his very best suit for looking at the paintings, but there was no conceivable way he could wear it out to lunch in the land of the Glimpses.

'Yes, I absolutely insist,' said Georgina. 'It's the least I can do. Now, my address is 17 Boltons Grove. It's just off The Boltons, garden flat. See you tomorrow.'

An hour later saw James in a state of wretched ecstasy in Austin Reed, his Barclaycard growing very warm in his pocket, buying a suit. He did seem to have good taste, he thought, and, more surprisingly, to be able to wear clothes well; in a dark-grey pinstripe and a white-and-grey striped shirt, he could hold his sartorial own against Jonathan any day. These at least he would be able to take home, Anne would never know what they'd cost, and then he could smuggle the shoes in a month or so later. He was beginning to enjoy the whole thing.

*   *   *

'Oh, hello,' said Georgina, dressed in a bath towel and looking slightly surprised as she opened the door to him next day (he had pleaded toothache in the office). 'Gosh, is that the time already? I've only just got up. Come in, would you like a coffee or something?'

'Yes please,' said James, looking round with interest. Georgina's flat was exactly as he had known it would be while at the same time being totally unpredictable (how uncomfortably well

30

he understood this new world. It was as if he had been a changeling, stolen away at birth by suburban fairies. He liked that thought; it charmed him and made him feel less guilty). White everywhere, with high ceilings and marble floors; in the drawing room an exquisite Indian carpet hung on one of the walls, two carved screens stood in either corner, and a heavy wrought-iron chandelier with tall white candles in it hung from the ceiling; a slightly surprising raspberry-pink sofa set in the window bay lent the room wit. There were two Chiparus bronzes, a Lalique brass lamp and an art nouveau rocking chair; two enormous ferns spilt out of a pair of pure white jardinières. James stood drinking it in, like a starving man; he could hardly tear his eyes from it even to go into the kitchen (all black and white, not a splinter of pine to be seen), where Georgina was calling to him to fetch his coffee.

'Could you bear to wait just three minutes while I get dressed?' she said. 'And then I'll show you the pictures.'

'Yes, that's fine,' said James. 'No hurry, really, you go ahead.' He would have waited three hours and happily, but in almost exactly three minutes she was back, wearing jeans and a grey silk shirt. She really was most beautiful: quite tall and very slim, her eyes so dark blue they were almost navy, her hair a wild blond mane. She could have been any age from eighteen to twenty-five; boldly he told her so, and she laughed.

'I'm just twenty-one. The flat was a birthday present; do you like it?'

'Very much, yes,' said James, anxious to appear as one to whom a flat in The Boltons was an absolutely standard birthday present. 'But where

31

are the paintings?'

'Oh, they're here,' she said, and dragged them out from under one of the sofas. 'Now what do you think? More coffee?'

'No thank you,' said James, looking at the pictures. They were fairly ordinary seascapes: pretty and a little unusual, but not worth more than £300 the pair.

'Oh dear, I can tell they're worthless, aren't they?' said Georgina.

'Well, not worthless, but not worth much,' said James truthfully. 'Not worth insuring separately anyway. You should just get them included on your existing policy.'

'Oh, damn, and I was so sure I'd made a real find,' said Georgina. 'Now that bastard Jonathan will laugh at me. Oh well, back to the drawing board. Gosh, it's nearly time for my class.'

James had been wondering what the class could be. Anne was always attending classes; as well as her course in self-awareness, she had done upholstery, child development and literary appreciation, none of which seemed likely Glimpse studies. He noticed that Georgina had a leotard lying over one of the chairs.

'Are you a dancer?' he asked.

'Oh heavens, no. I'm an art dealer very manqué. As you can see. No, I go to dance class every day to keep my weight down. Now I haven't forgotten about lunch; I still want to take you. Could you meet me at San Fred's at one fifteen? Please. Don't argue. Just come.'

San Frediano was Glimpse country all right. Pretty, careless people sat at tables with other pretty, careless people, frequently darting across the room to greet, to kiss, to exclaim still more. James arrived deliberately early and sat at the table Georgina had thoughtfully booked, watching and absorbing. He was a quick study; in the twenty minutes he spent there, he learnt a great deal about the group behaviour and sexual signalling of the breed he was scrutinising. When Georgina arrived, he took her hand and kissed her cheek. 'I missed you,' he said.

'Do you know,' she said, sparkling up at him, 'I don't even know your name.'

'My name,' said James, sipping a glass of champagne he had taken it upon himself to order, 'is James. What else would you like to know?'

*   *   *

Two hours later they were both rather drunk. Georgina had knocked over two glasses of wine and spilt her sauce down her silk shirt; she sat with her thigh pressed hard against James's, her hand moving rather agitatedly in his and her dark blue eyes fixed on his grey ones with some degree of intensity.

'Tell me,' she said. 'Could your company manage without you for another hour or so? Because I don't think I can.'

'Oh yes,' said James. 'I'm quite sure it could. Let's get a taxi.'

*   *   *

In the taxi, he felt suddenly nervous. The strictly paced, absolutely predictable routine he went through with Anne every six days was the only

33

sexual experience he had known for many years; he did not feel it really equipped him to move the earth or even a tiny bit of The Boltons with this beautiful, hungry person.

Undressing (and oh dear, he thought, more anxiously wretched than ever, the shirt and suit might be Austin Reed, but the vest and Y-fronts were Marks & Spencer and a baggy three years old at that), he felt worse and worse, and became totally silent, feeling foolish.

But Georgina did not seem to be caring very much, either about the Y-fronts or the silence. She lay on her bed (even in his hour of trial he noticed that the head of it was cast iron, art nouveau and undoubtedly worth a fortune), her own slightly too skinny body absolutely naked, and held out her arms as he lay down and kissed her forehead in a gesture of extraordinary sweetness. What followed was quite outside his experience in levels of passion and delight, but he did not feel clumsy or nervous; it was as if some powerfully invading sexual force had entered him that he might enter her. It was a triumph and a glory and afterwards he thought that for the first time he had truly understood what it meant to make love.

'Goodness me,' said Georgina, as they lay smiling at one another. 'I hope your company has a good policy out on you.'

'I'm afraid,' said James with perfect truth, 'that they wouldn't mind if I died tomorrow.'

'Oh, nonsense,' said Georgina. 'I'm sure they must be hugely dependent on you. Now listen, I have to go in about ten minutes, to the gallery to see some idiot painter with Jonathan. And you, I suppose, have to go back to your important job and then home to your lovely, kind, maternal wife.'

'I'm afraid I do,' said James, thinking with some dread of the metamorphosis that had to be gone through before he got home; rather like a speeded-up film, he watched himself phoning from a call box—'Tooth out, really painful, going straight home'—the tube journey to Paddington, the exchange of his new shoes for his old at the left-luggage office (the suit was quite enough to explain for one week), the dreary trundle home on the 6.13, having killed a couple of hours in the buffet bar, and then 'hello-darling-had-a-good-day-need-any-help-up-there' as he got into bath time, story time and babysitting while Anne went to fulfil her duties as treasurer of the Residents' Association.

It was all right at first; he thought himself dutifully into his proper role—or rather improper, as he increasingly felt it to be—towelled down small plump bodies (to the accompaniment of some disturbing images of a larger skinny one), read *Winnie the Pooh* and dutifully ate sausages and mash despite his taste buds being still tuned to quails' eggs and champagne. Later, he helped Anne make lanterns for the shepherds in the nativity play, commiserated with her over being landed with making all the quiches for the PTA supper and barn dance, and fell asleep in front of the television while she was out. But later, when she had come back and was making their bedtime cocoa, he remembered with a thud of anxiety that this was the sixth, if not the seventh night, and the Laura Ashley nightie would undoubtedly be unbuttoned. It was; he closed his eyes and thought of The Boltons and got through it somehow. Not splendidly, but just about competently; afterwards he mumbled something about being tired and fell into a confused sleep. Life might be beautiful amongst the Glimpses, but it was dreadfully demanding.

*   *   *

And expensive too, he thought, looking aghast at his Barclaycard statement two months later. From a fairly respectable £1,000 at the beginning of December, it had now soared to a very nasty-looking £8,500, with a note at the bottom that said, 'Do not use your card further without authority' and a list of purchases that would have made a wonderful case for a prosecuting divorce lawyer. Clothes, meals, flowers and wine all sat upon it in extravagant splendour; the suitcase in the left-luggage office was bursting at its tacky seams.

He was worried all the time; he worried about money, worried about his job (which he was neglecting terribly), worried about his marriage; he was perpetually tired, chronically confused (who am I today, this morning, tomorrow night), and permanently and rapturously happy.

For the impossible had happened and he and Georgina had fallen in love. He had not known love before, he realised; had not experienced the delicate uncurling of tenderness, the steady, powerful growth of joy, the insistent pounding of desire, the explosion of need to be with the beloved every available moment of every existing hour. What he had felt for Anne had been a decorous, carefully chosen piece of furniture for his life; what he knew for Georgina was a total demolition of everything that could be deemed right and

36

proper and a restructure into new, beautiful, unrecognisable territory.

At first he had not been able to believe that she loved him in return, had thought she must be simply amusing herself, but she did, she told him so day after dizzy day, growing paler and even thinner while assuring him of her happiness and her contentment with the way things were. She had given up Jonathan, she had stopped wanting to go to parties; she simply waited, infinitely patient, for the times they could be together.

James found the transition from one life to the other more and more difficult to make, the contrast increasingly painful and sharp. Although he had stopped pretending totally to Georgina, had told her some of the truth (that he did not actually quite belong with the Glimpses, that he was not in fact very important or rich), he still felt and indeed became metamorphosed when he was with her into somebody quite different, somebody in whom he was beginning rather dangerously to believe.

Every meeting, every lunch, every rare outing put him further in love, but it did something else too, more ridiculous, less innocent: it made him more deeply committed to, more totally besotted with, Georgina's lifestyle. And he had no right to that; he had earned her, perhaps, by way of words and loving and lovemaking, but not the rest. He was helplessly, hopelessly in debt, and worse than in debt, in thrall. The Glimpses had become sorcerers; they had cast a spell on him, and he could not escape.

*   *   *

The crunch came, of course; it had to, sneaking up on him like some sinister, predatory beast.

It was not a love letter that gave him away, as they do in books, nor a well-meaning friend, as they do in real life; not even his Barclaycard statement, his diary or the labels on his new shirts. It was a ticket from the left-luggage office at Paddington station.

The children found it; they were fiddling with his wallet one Saturday morning, as he tried rather wearily to concentrate on what Anne was telling him about the new Neighbourhood Watch scheme, and he realised too late that they had actually extracted the ticket, along with a five-pound note and his driving licence, and were playing a game of cards with them all on the table.

'Children, give those to me, at once,' he said, just a little too sharply. Anne looked up, aware of the urgency in his tone, saw the expression on his face, and then looked down at the table.

'What on earth have you got in the left-luggage office?' she said.

'Oh, nothing. Nothing much,' said James. He was sweating; he reached out for the coffee pot and tried to control his shaking hand.

'What do you mean, nothing? Why should you have anything there? Why can't you tell me?'

'Of course I can tell you. It's just, well, my briefcase. With some rather important work in. There's nowhere I can keep anything safe in this bloody shambles. I put it there for the weekend.'

'James, don't be ridiculous. You've got the office. You're lying. What on earth is in the left-luggage office at Paddington station that you can't tell me about?'

'Oh, darling,' said James, in a last desperate attempt to escape from the vice that was holding him. 'Just some work. And—and some wine,' he added, beginning to stammer. 'Some wine for next Thursday, when your parents are coming round. I couldn't carry it, so I left it until I had the car. All right?'

'No,' said Anne. 'Not all right. You're still lying. And if you won't tell me what's there, I want to go and see for myself.' She was flushed and breathing very heavily; her eyes were brilliant and fixed on his face.

'I'm going to Paddington,' she said. 'Now. Do you want to come with me or not?' James nodded helplessly. 'Come along, children, we're all going out.'

They drove to Paddington in silence. The children were quiet, sensing a drama. James felt terribly sick. There was nothing now that he could do. Anne was going to open Pandora's box in the middle of Paddington station, and the demons inside were deadly indeed.

They didn't look deadly, just rather odd. Three silk shirts, two of them slightly smelly; a suit; two pairs of shoes; a jacket; a Gucci wallet and cashmere sweater. Anne looked at them, looked at him, and then picked out the wallet. Inside was a bill for lunch at the Savoy, and a note in Georgina's handwriting. 'Thank you for the best two hours of my whole life,' it read.

'You creep,' was all she said, and then she walked away to the car with the children, leaving James to journey home alone on the train.

He did think of ringing Georgina, but it seemed a messy point to do it at. He preferred to wait until at least something had been resolved.

When he finally got home, Anne was making bread, as she always did when she was worried or upset; indeed, the smell of baking, far from typifying calm and comfort to James, always meant trouble, ranging in severity from a difficult committee meeting to a bad attack of PMT. He stood silent, waiting for her to speak.

'I don't want to talk about it now,' she said, very cold and calm. 'We'll wait until the children are in bed.'

'The children?' he said. 'Don't you think this is more important than the children?'

She looked at him with such dislike, such contempt that his knees literally gave way beneath him and he had to sit down. 'I personally don't think anything is more important than the children,' she said, 'and certainly not your squalid, well-dressed adultery.'

She had always had a way with words.

*   *   *

'I have decided,' said Anne, finally sitting down that evening with a glass of wine and a very determined expression, 'that the best thing is for you to stay, at least for a while, so we can work things out. There's no point acting hastily. Obviously I am partly to blame; this sort of thing is never just one person's fault. I am quite happy to talk it through and find out what's gone wrong, and see what we can do to put things right again.'

I should be feeling grateful, thought James, wondering why he wasn't. I should be kissing her feet, saying I'm sorry, begging for forgiveness. But

40

I'm not.

'I don't want to hear about her,' Anne went on. 'I can't see the point. In fact, I'd rather not. As long as you promise me never to see her again, then that can be the end of her as far as I'm concerned. I've no wish to know what she looks like or what she does, or what she has to offer. I can't see what good it would do. Obviously it's been a difficult time for you, but we must just try to put it behind us. You can't undo the past, after all.'

James looked at her sitting there, smiling carefully, not crying, not applying emotional blackmail, in her cosy battered chair where she had breastfed and cuddled and comforted the children, and mended their clothes and made out lists for Sainsbury's and written minutes of meetings, good Anne, kind Anne, well-organised, loyal, blind Anne, and he knew that he had to tell her, that there was no point trying to be kind, attempting to spare her, selling her a soft option. He had to dish up the truth, raw, unseasoned, unpalatable, and force her to swallow it.

'I'm sorry,' he said, 'but you have to hear about her. About all of it. I just have to tell you. You have to understand.'

Anne stopped looking determined and started looking nervous. She had found a once-fluffy pink rabbit stuffed down her chair, and she started picking at its bare patches, making them bigger, less neat. James looked at it and thought it symbolised their marriage, getting balder and more hideous every moment.

'To start with,' he said, 'I can't possibly promise never to see her again. I love her. I'm sorry, but I can't help it and that's the fact of the matter. And

41

more important probably is for you to hear what she has to offer. That will do some good, because it will make you see why we can't put things right. What Georgina—that's her name—what she has to offer is a way of life. The way of life I need, that suits me. The life we've been sharing, you and I, is not right for me. I know that now. And I can't stay in it. It's stifling me. I need something more—well, more adult.'

'I see,' said Anne. She was looking at him with an odd expression that was half distaste, half something quite different. Had James been a little less overwrought, he might have recognised it as humour.

'That is precisely what Georgina has to offer me, you see,' he said. 'An adult life. A life with some beauty in it. A selfish life, if you like. But it is the only life I can bear to lead now. I am desperately sorry. I can see I must seem hideously ungrateful, and you shall have every penny I can possibly give you. I shall visit the children if you will let me whenever I can, but I can't go on living here.'

Anne gazed at him blankly for a while, and then said, 'I see,' for a second time. That was the end of their marriage.

*   *   *

It was not that neat and tidy, of course. The hostilities actually went on for some time. Anne's calm exploded into a noisy, anguished outrage, and James's cool reason deserted him from time to time; but at the end of it they met; they gazed at each other over the dreadful irony of the head of their youngest child, awakened by the noise and

42

now asleep again on his mother's lap, and managed to smile, exhaustedly, weakly, but at least not entirely estranged.

Anne then took the child to bed with her, closing the door gently behind her; and so, his marriage seeming to him thus most poignantly epitomised, James walked very quietly out of the door, got into the car and drove to Georgina's flat.

He stopped on the way to phone her, to tell her no more than that he was coming; she had some friends with her, but promised to get rid of them before he arrived, and he feasted his mind desperately on her, and how he would find her, how he needed to find her.

The journey he was making symbolised the whole of his past life: away from the laurel hedges, the gravel drives, the estate cars, the quiet, safe streets, and into the dazzling, hustling busyness of Saturday-night London. He had left the womb he had inhabited for so long, so warm, so cosy, so increasingly uncomfortable, and been thrust into a new, bright, hard-edged world where he might be fighting for his life, but where at least the life was what he wanted. He knew it wasn't going to remain so simple, so clear-cut; there would be endless journeys back to the womb, half-felt regrets. There would be dreadful financial difficulties, legal unpleasantness and sorrowing faces, and the loss of much love. But for this hour, this night, he allowed himself the luxury of seeing it simply, of having chosen what he wanted, done battle for it and won.

Tonight he would be where he belonged, cleaved finally to the Glimpses: in a white flat in Kensington with not a carton of Ribena in a half-mile radius, where the Fisher-Prices were the nice new couple at number 92 and the only cries in the night were adult and orgasmic.

Exhausted and exalted, he reached The Boltons, parked the car, ran down the steps, rang the bell. Georgina fell into his arms; beyond her stood paradise, quiet, peaceful, beautiful . . .

'What is it?' she said. 'What has happened? Tell me, tell me everything.'

'I've done it,' he said weakly, collapsing on to the pink sofa. 'I've left her. I'm here to stay. If you'll have me.'

'Oh my darling,' said Georgina. 'As if I wouldn't.' She paused and looked at him, her navy-blue eyes huge and starry. 'I have some wonderful news too. I'm going to have a baby . . .'

THE BEST TABLE

You didn't expect to feel socially inferior on a bus, Belinda thought, but she certainly felt it on this one. It was called the Hampton Jitney, and it was filled with people leaving New York City for the weekend heaven of the Hamptons, dressed in cashmere sweaters and goodness-knew-whose jeans, their Louis Vuitton and Gucci weekend bags slung up on the luggage rack together with their Ralph Lauren overcoats. They all seemed to know one another, and were discussing who was going to stay with whom and which parties they might be going to, over the coffee and orange juice and admittedly rather soggy croissants that had just been served. Belinda wasn't wearing cashmere, but M&S lambswool under a Gap body warmer, and her weekend bag came from T. K. Maxx.

Belinda was in New York for a fortnight; it was her first trip, and in some ways it had been a disappointment. Of course the city was wonderful, and she had done all the touristy things, the Empire State and the ice rink at the Rockefeller Center and the Circle Line tour, but she had done them alone, and her evenings had been mostly spent in her hotel room, after an early foray into the bar. It had seemed a rather good idea initially; she had been depressed after a relationship which had gone very wrong, and an advertisement for bargain packages to 'do your Christmas shopping in the Big Apple' had caught her eye. That was what she needed: a bit of excitement in her life. She had enlisted her best friend Sarah as travelling companion, but Sarah had developed an appalling flu virus two days before departure, and it was too late to find anyone else, so Belinda had decided to go alone. She was bound to befriend someone, if not on the flight, then at the hotel.

But the plane had been packed with couples or middle-aged women travelling together; no one remotely suitable for a single girl of twenty-four to explore the Big Apple with. Not even the tours the rep organised had produced anyone. And so, the major sights seen, Belinda had walked the streets of the city, checked out the stores and seen a couple of movies—all alone. New York was a very forbidding place, she had discovered, if you didn't know anybody. She was actually counting the days until her return to London when Sarah called.

'It's fantastic,' Belinda had lied, 'absolutely amazing. I've done so much. It's—well, wonderful.'

'Oh, God. It's so unfair. Now, do you have any

spare time this weekend?'

'Um—possibly. Why?'

'Well, I was talking to Rachel—you know . . . yes, you do, that girl in marketing with the huge boobs—and she's got an aunt who lives in the Hamptons, that wonderful place where they all have summer houses, Spielberg and—and—well, everybody. The houses all cost about twenty million dollars.'

'Oh,' said Belinda. It sounded even less welcoming than New York City.

'But Rachel's aunt doesn't live in one of those; she just has a little house. Her husband owns a bookstore or something. Anyway, Rachel spoke to her and she said she'd just love you to go and visit them this weekend. I think they're quite lonely; their children have left home, and you know what Americans are like, so hospitable—well of course you do.'

'Yes, of course.'

'So give her a ring. She'll be really pleased. Now, they're called the Hunters, and . . .'

Mrs Hunter had the warmest, kindliest voice Belinda had heard since leaving England.

'Come on Saturday morning and stay. We're very quiet these days, so I hope it won't be dull for you.'

'Well, I really don't feel I should impose on you . . .' said Belinda carefully. 'Maybe just lunch or something.'

'Oh no, dear, it's much too far to come just for lunch. You stay. Get the eight a.m. Jitney, book to East Hampton and then call us. I'm only just down the road; I'll come and pick you up.'

*　　　*　　　*

46

'Hi,' said a voice. 'Mind if I sit here?'

Belinda blinked; she had dozed off. An extremely attractive man was smiling down at her, wearing the obligatory grey cashmere sweater, washed-out jeans and boat shoes. He had dark hair and very intense dark eyes, and a sweetly diffident smile. He looked a bit like George Clooney, she thought confusedly.

'Of course not. No, please sit down. I haven't missed my stop, have I?'

'Where is your stop?'

'East Hampton.'

'Mine too. It's about another fifteen minutes. I'm sorry to disturb you, but I've been sitting on the wheel and it's making me feel sick. I saw the space next to you and . . .'

'You're not disturbing me at all. Please do sit down.'

He was easy to talk to. He was going to stay with a friend, he said. 'I don't often get away at the weekend.'

'What do you do?'

'Oh, I . . . well, I own a restaurant in downtown Manhattan.'

'That must be fun.'

'Occasionally. Mostly it's one huge slog. Especially on Saturdays. It's a treat to get out of the city. What do you do?'

'I work for a law firm. In London.'

'Oh, really? Are you one of those high-powered City types? Or do you wear one of those white wigs?'

'I wish. Neither. I'm just a trainee.'

She asked him about the restaurant, what he did there.

47

'Oh—a bit of everything. A little cooking, a little admin. You should come down. Now look, here we are at East Hampton.'

It was an absurdly perfect place, with very white houses, very green lawns, and a gleaming pond overhung with large but very tidy willows and home to what appeared to be perfectly groomed ducks.

'When does the hero come on?' she said, laughing.

'Pardon me?'

'It's like something from *The Truman Show*.'

'I guess it is. Here's the stop,' he said, hauling his Gucci holdall down, and handing her her T. K. Maxx one. 'You OK now? Anyone meeting you?'

'I have to phone . . . Oh God, no! Oh, how stupid of me, my phone's out of juice.'

'Use mine.'

He insisted on waiting until Mrs Hunter arrived: 'I was brought up to look after maidens in distress.'

'I'm not in distress any more,' she said. 'You've looked after me perfectly.'

'Well, it's an excuse to talk a bit longer,' he said. 'Here, have my card. This is the restaurant number. Give them my name, then you're sure to get a good table.'

'Richard Korda', the card said, and the restaurant was called Lloyds Café, on East 15th, very far from the glamour of mid-town Manhattan. It didn't sound like the sort of place you'd have trouble getting a table, Belinda thought. He was probably just trying to impress her. She smiled at him, shook his hand.

'I'm Belinda,' she said. 'Belinda Ward.'

'I'll remember that. What a pretty name. Maybe I'll see you on the way back. I'm catching the five.'

48

'Oh—no, I'm on the three o'clock,' she said, wondering wildly if you could change a Jitney ticket.

'Oh, OK. Well, enjoy the rest of your trip.' He hesitated, then, 'Look, would you like to meet for coffee or brunch or something in the morning? Give me your friend's number.'

This really is like a film, she thought, meeting someone handsome and charming. And on a bus.

The Hunters were unpretentious, intensely welcoming. After lunch, Mary Hunter took her for a drive, showing her the sights of the Hamptons, the astonishing mansions, the wild ocean and shore, the charm of Sag Harbor, where they had their bookstore. They lived in what seemed to Belinda a fairly modest house on the outskirts of East Hampton; later she learned that it was worth at least five million dollars.

They were eating an early supper when the phone rang. Richard Korda, Belinda thought wildly.

But, 'That was Francesca, our youngest daughter,' said Mary. 'I told her you were here, and she says to be sure to call her tomorrow and she'll meet you for a drink.'

If only she'd met these nice people earlier, Belinda thought.

*   *   *

Richard Korda did ring, but to say that he'd got involved with 'a business thing. So I'm sorry, can't make brunch. But be sure to come down to the restaurant, won't you? And . . . could I maybe call you when I come to London next month?'

49

'Of course,' she said. 'That would be lovely.' She gave him her number, and was about to say that she wouldn't have time to come to the restaurant, that tomorrow was her last night and she was committed to Francesca, when he said, 'Sorry, got to go. Bye, Belinda. Nice talking to you.'

*   *   *

Francesca was very New York: dark, self-confident, very, very thin. She worked in an art gallery and lived in a loft in the Village. Belinda felt rather awed by her, and thanked her for finding the time to meet her.

'Oh, I've got nothing else to do this evening,' Francesca said tactlessly, sipping at her cocktail. 'I've been working on this guy, Drew Balfour; he exhibits at our gallery, but I can't make him notice me. I hope you weren't too bored over the weekend,' she added. 'My parents are sweet, but not exactly exciting. I don't expect you met anyone under fifty.'

'It was great,' said Belinda truthfully. 'I really enjoyed it. And actually,' she said, anxious to appear marginally more interesting, 'I did meet someone. On the Jitney. He owns a restaurant in Manhattan and—'

'Yeah? Which one?'

'Oh, I'm sure you won't have heard of it,' said Belinda. 'It's called . . . oh yes, Lloyds Café. On . . .' she rummaged for Richard Korda's card, 'on East 15th.'

'Lloyds? My God,' said Francesca, snatching the card. 'That is one of the hottest tickets in town right now. Waiting lists for a table are as long as your

50

arm.'

'Well, he said to mention his name if I called,' said Belinda, slightly defensively, taking it back, 'and he'd make sure I got one.'

'You are kidding! My God, how cool is that? Richard Korda in person! What was he like? Totally up himself, I suppose?'

'No,' said Belinda. 'He was absolutely lovely. I really liked him. He asked me to brunch.'

'He did? Where did you go?'

'Well, nowhere in the end,' said Belinda reluctantly. 'He didn't have time. But he was really sweet and—'

'Sweet? I don't think so. I can tell you've only been in New York five minutes. Did he tell you about his wife?'

'Well—no.'

'Very nasty divorce. He tried to get out of the pre-nup, and . . .'

Belinda felt rather depressed suddenly. Depressed and silly, thinking Richard Korda had actually liked her.

Just the same, she should have gone to his restaurant, she thought, not wasted her last night like this. Maybe even now: but then Francesca would want to go with her. Which didn't seem the best idea . . .

Rather regretfully, she ordered another cocktail and then went back to the hotel to pack. Putting any sentimental thoughts about Richard Korda firmly out of her head.

*   *   *

The month passed, and then six weeks; there was

51

no call from Richard Korda. Well, as if he would. She felt silly for even thinking it was a possibility. He was a cool New York restaurateur and she was a rather uncool trainee solicitor.

It was June. Alan Robinson, Belinda's boss, had to go to New York to work out the final details of a corporate deal.

'I think I might take you with me,' he said. 'There's going to be a lot of legwork, and it'd be great experience for you. How would you feel about it?'

'Pretty good,' she said, smiling. 'Great, in fact.'

It wouldn't be as glamorous as it sounded, she knew; mostly she'd be sitting in meetings and hotel rooms and writing up endless minutes. But it was still New York. And at least she wouldn't be alone this time. Sarah was frantic with jealousy.

'Twice! It's so unfair. Now mind you go and look that guy up this time. The one at the restaurant.'

'Sarah! I couldn't. Not after all this time. He'll have forgotten who I am. And—'

'Course he won't. Nothing ventured and all that. Promise me.'

'All right,' said Belinda, crossing her fingers, 'I promise.'

Working in New York was actually more fun than not working. They stayed at the Plaza, and the New York partner insisted she join them for dinner the first night. After that there was no going out; they worked until after midnight twice and one night until six a.m. But it was exciting; she felt like a real *Sex and the City* girl, as if she belonged there.

They were going home the next day. Alan was having dinner with friends. 'Can you amuse yourself?'

'Oh—yes,' said Belinda happily. A couple of the girls from the office had offered to take her out if she had time.

But then at the last minute the arrangement fell through. Disappointed, she was rummaging through her wallet, checking how many dollars she had left, when Richard Korda's card fell out.

Could she? No, she couldn't.

She could hear Sarah's voice upbraiding her: 'You didn't even try! You total wimp.'

Belinda poured herself a Martini from the minibar and picked up the phone.

*   *   *

The girl was coolly regretful.

'I'm sorry, Mr Korda says no, he absolutely doesn't have a table for you.'

She was taken aback by the hostility of the message. Well, at least she'd tried. How stupid to think he would have remembered her. How pathetic. Anyway, she'd be perfectly happy having a club sandwich from room service and going to bed early. She was really tired . . .

*   *   *

Their plane wasn't leaving till late afternoon. Belinda thought she might go for a walk, take a look around at some of the areas she hadn't seen before.

'Go to the Lower East Side,' said Alan. 'It's fun down there. I've got some emails to send, or I'd go with you.'

It wasn't as if it was her idea. She was only taking

his advice.

*   *   *

At midday, she found herself on the corner of East 15th. Well, it would be silly not to at least have a look at Lloyds Café. Just out of interest. And obviously, he wouldn't be there.

It was really extremely cool-looking. All white tiles, ceiling to floor, and the tables stainless steel, with mirrors running down both sides, and the cooking area at the back open to the restaurant, with great steel hoods to absorb the steam.

Maybe she should just have a drink there. So she could tell Sarah.

*   *   *

She was sipping at her mojito when he came in with a sheaf of menus. He saw her, did a double-take, then obviously recognised her. He smiled at her, rather coolly and she took a deep breath.

'Hi, I don't suppose you remember me. It's Belinda, from . . .' He really wasn't looking very friendly at all. Hostile even. Why? 'From the Jitney. No, of course you wouldn't.'

'I do remember you,' he said briefly. 'Of course I do.'

'Oh, you do? Well, I'm in New York, working. I was at a loose end, and I thought I'd come and have a look at your restaurant. It's really nice.'

'Thank you.'

She smiled at him, nervously. He didn't smile back. Maybe he had taken it personally, her not coming earlier.

54

'I—I so wanted to come before,' she said, 'but there just wasn't time.'

'Oh, really?'

'Well—yes. I had to go home. Plane to catch, you know.' She smiled at him again.

He shrugged. Belinda began to feel cross. Did he really expect people to miss planes just to eat in his silly restaurant? This was arrogant, even by New York standards. She felt rather sorry for the wife in her fight over the pre-nup. Clearly Francesca had been right: Richard Korda was totally up himself. And to think she'd nursed romantic thoughts about him. She had to get out of here.

She looked round for the waiter, signalled to him for the bill.

'You must excuse me,' Richard Korda said, and walked away to the back of the restaurant.

She was just signing the card receipt when she heard her name.

'Is that you, Belinda? What on earth are you doing here?'

It was Francesca; Francesca and a flashy-looking man with dyed blond hair, a toning leather jacket and very small round glasses with dense black lenses.

'I'm visiting New York on business. With my boss.'

'Are you? Nice one. And you thought you'd finally try out Lloyds. We come here every Saturday for brunch, don't we, Drew?'

So she'd managed to get him after all, Belinda thought.

Drew nodded briefly, then pulled a ringing phone out of his pocket. He clearly didn't feel it necessary to waste any time on Belinda. He walked

55

to the doorway, talking, studying himself in the mirrors as he went.

'Isn't he great?' said Francesca, looking at him. 'So, so cool. We're getting a place together soon.' She smiled at Belinda. 'You know, I really should buy you a drink. It was a real turning point, that introduction of yours. It made such an impression on Drew, me getting a table at Lloyds. He really looked at me for the first time.'

'What introduction?' said Belinda, after the briefest reflection that if that was what it took to ensnare the unpleasant Drew, he obviously wasn't worth having. 'I don't understand.'

'Well, I rang up, used your name. So I could be sure to get the table.'

'You what?' said Belinda. She suddenly felt violently angry. 'Francesca, that was so wrong of you. Terribly dishonest.'

'Oh, for heaven's sake,' said Francesca impatiently. 'You sound like something out of *Little Women*. You weren't going to use it; you were going back to England. What difference did it make?'

'A lot, to me,' said Belinda. 'And Richard Korda seems pretty upset as well. He obviously thinks I just told you to do it.'

'Well, and what if he does? What's that to you?'

Drew returned, smoothing his hair. 'We need to get on, babe. I've got a full schedule today.'

'Excuse me,' said Belinda, turning her back on them.

She walked towards the back of the restaurant, to the door Richard Korda had gone through.

'I'm sorry,' said the girl sitting at a table checking names on a list. 'You can't go through there.'

'I have to,' said Belinda. 'I need to see Mr

56

Korda.'

'I'm afraid that won't be possible,' said the girl, going back to her list.

'Well, I'll just have to wait.'

The girl shrugged. Belinda felt astonished at her own courage. Her only other emotion was to think how much she was beginning to dislike New Yorkers.

After about ten minutes, the door opened and Richard Korda came out. He looked at her with the same blank expression.

'She says she has to see you,' said the girl.

'I'm sorry. I'm very busy.'

'I can see that. And I have a plane to catch. Look, it's important.'

He sighed. 'All right. Let's sit down.'

He led her to a table at the back.

'Look, I just wanted to say, I had no idea she was going to do that. Francesca, I mean.'

'What? Who?'

'That other girl. Use my name, pretend she was me to get a table. It was an awful thing to do. I can't quite believe it.'

He said nothing; just continued to look at her blankly.

'I'm so sorry,' she said. She looked over at their table, where Drew was complaining loudly that his eggs weren't sufficiently soft. 'I really had no idea.'

'I see,' said Richard. Still the blank look.

'So . . . so that's all really. I just wanted to set the record straight. I wondered why you didn't call me when you came to London. Now I must go. I have a plane to catch, like I said.'

'You were expecting me to call you?'

'Well . . . yes. Hoping you would anyway,' she

57

said, and then felt foolish and hurried on. 'I'm not surprised now that you didn't.'

She stood up. He was staring at her again, saying nothing. Belinda began to feel irritated. Some kind of response might have been nice. Like 'I'm so glad to know that', or 'I really appreciate your telling me'.

It didn't come.

There was a sudden commotion from Drew's table. He was shouting at the waiter, saying he had ordered Badoit, not Evian.

'That man,' said Richard Korda. 'I'd like to have him banned from the restaurant. I'm sorry, I know he's a friend of yours, but . . .'

'He's no friend of mine, and I think he should be banned from the planet,' said Belinda. 'Now, if you'll excuse me . . .'

She turned and walked towards the door. She had to get away, away from these ridiculous people, safely back to nice English Alan at the hotel.

And then, as she reached the sidewalk, she felt a hand on her shoulder and turned to see Richard Korda standing in front of her. He was looking different; gentler. 'I'm sorry, but did you say he's not a friend of yours?'

'Of course he's not. I think he's absolutely awful.' Now she was sounding like an English schoolgirl. This was getting worse.

'I'm sorry,' he said again. 'I've—well, I've made a bit of a mistake. Look—I didn't care about the table, Belinda. That sort of thing happens all the time. People will do anything to get a table here. God knows why. I guessed right away.'

'Oh,' she said, staring at him. 'But I don't understand. Why—why were you so cross with me in that case?'

'I suppose,' he said slowly, 'it was that you could know such awful people. I thought you were really special when I met you, fresh and different. I was absurdly pleased when I thought you were coming in and absurdly disappointed when you didn't. I had champagne ready to bring to the table, and—'

'Oh,' she said, 'oh, Richard, I'm so sorry.'

'Oh, it was ridiculous of me. And if they'd been nice people, people like you, I wouldn't have minded nearly so much. I suppose I felt let down. Not by you, but by life in general. The thing is, I'm in rather a bad way at the moment, Belinda. Going through a very nasty divorce.'

She hoped she looked surprised. 'I'm sorry.'

'I get easily depressed. I'm scared of everything. Everybody.'

'I'm so sorry,' she said again. So this was the brush-off. He was simply letting her down very lightly.

And then, 'Look,' he said, 'why don't you come back in and have that brunch at long last? Better late than never. If you've got time, of course. And I could make sure,' he added, and smiled quite easily now, 'that you get a really good table. In fact, the best.'

THE MERMAID

He really didn't like her. She was too—shiny. Everything about her shone: her lipstick, her nails, her jewellery—she had a lot of that—her shoes. She had perfect, shiny white teeth, and shiny swingy hair, and her skin was all golden, and gleamy too. He had a bit of trouble not liking her car, which was parked outside the house and which was very shiny indeed; it was silver and it had a top which let down—exactly the sort of car he would have loved if it had been his dad's. But it wasn't, it was hers. She offered to take him for a ride in it, with the top down, but he shook his head.

'Surely you'd like that?' his dad said. 'It'd be really good fun.' He winked at him. 'Martin'd see you; he's out on his bike.'

Martin lived in the same street, and went to the same school and was in the same class, and boasted about everything: his skateboard, his computer, his bike, his mobile phone, his DVD player, his trainers. His dad didn't have a convertible car though. It'd be pretty cool to drive past in one. But not even that was enough to persuade him. It really hurt, but he shook his head.

He refused a meal at TGI's as well. He said he didn't like burgers any more.

'News to me,' said his father.

'I don't like them much either,' she said. 'How about a Chinese?'

He shook his head. 'I'm not hungry.'

'Jake,' said his dad, 'you're always hungry.'

'I'm not today.'

*   *   *

Julie went home alone, fairly early, feeling depressed. She couldn't have tried harder. Little beast. Sizing her up, deciding what to do about her. He always did that, Nick had said: 'You mustn't mind.'

60

She had said of course she didn't mind, but she did. She wasn't sure she liked the 'always' either. How many girlfriends had Nick taken home, for God's sake? Anyway, it really rankled . . . being rejected by a nine-year-old. Thoroughly rejected. She'd been so sure she could impress him. Impressing was what she did; it was her job. Impressing clients, getting their business; she hadn't got to be head of New Business at Farquar and Fanshawe by being unimpressive, now, had she? She'd realised, of course, this was quite a different game, but she had a nephew just about Jake's age and she knew the way to his heart. It was a pretty predictable path: new toys (not that what they played with these days could be dignified by the label of toy), rides in the car, trips to theme parks and lots of junk food. Only Jake's heart was clearly not to be found that way. Nick had warned her it might not be, of course: 'He's still grieving for Mary. And he's a funny little chap. Bit of an oddball.'

*   *   *

Mary, Jake's mother, had died two years earlier of ovarian cancer. She had been the perfect earth-mother, it seemed: bread-baking, patchwork-making, sweetly content at home, caring for her little family. Jake's room still bore testimony to it: three walls and the entire ceiling covered with pictures that she had painted, forests and waterfalls and night skies and, Jake's favourite, a wonderful under-sea scene, with a mermaid sitting on a rock, looking into a mirror as she combed her hair. He talked to the mermaid, when he felt really bad, told her how unhappy he was, and how terribly he missed his mother. He knew it was silly, but it seemed to help, and it meant he didn't have to say those sorts of things to his father and make him even more worried than he already was.

Mary had been a piano teacher, and Jake had been an immensely promising player himself; but since her death he had refused even to touch the piano, and had made his father keep it locked.

Julie had said (through slightly gritted teeth) that she would have expected Mary to have had more children. 'She couldn't,' Nick had said with a sigh.

She was secretly pleased; at least there was something Mary hadn't been good at.

*   *   *

Nick was not surprised by Jake's reaction to Julie. It was always the same. (He regretted that 'always'. It had just slipped out, making it seem as if he had had dozens of girlfriends, when there had only been a couple.) But he was very disappointed. He could see that he was only one step away from falling in love with this one. She was so—lovely. So pretty, and clever and funny, yet, underneath that, so really . . . well, nice. Gentle and concerned and that wonderful word Mary had used a lot, *simpatico*.

She had seemed to be really sorry when he told her about Mary; sorry and concerned.

'It must be so hard,' she said, 'coping with everything and being unhappy as well. It's exhausting, being unhappy.'

She had been married herself; married and divorced.

'It was—messy,' she said, twisting a strand of her

shining brown hair round her finger. 'Messy and . . . just horrible. It still hurts.'

*   *   *

Initially, Nick had thought that never again would he so much as look at another woman, but somehow, as the worst of the grief eased and the loneliness intensified, he had wanted to have someone again. Not to marry, not even to be serious about, but just to talk to, be with, have fun with, and yes, all right, possibly a bit more than that. He knew Mary wouldn't have minded; quite the reverse. She had made him promise to at least consider marrying again. 'One day. You'll need someone. And so will Jake.'

Sure that he never would, he had promised. It seemed to calm her. She had been agitated, fretting over his loneliness, his inability to cope.

He had coped, of course. He'd had to. Coped with the grief, the anger, with Jake's grief and anger, and doing all the things Mary had done. He learned to shop and cook, to wash and iron, to go to parents' evenings, to get the school uniform organised on Sunday nights, the lunch box every morning. It was a little easier for him than it might be for most men, because he was a teacher: the hours fitted around Jake's life. He had even, this year, managed a birthday party. He was pretty proud of that. His sister had offered to do it for him; he had refused, almost indignantly.

'I can do it myself. And Jake wants me to.'

Jake had been so good: so brave and good. And such a companion to him. They had done everything together—at first. Walked, cycled, listened to music, watched TV, gone to the cinema, and talked and talked and talked.

'I love you so much, Dad,' Jake had said one night. 'Not more than Mum, I don't mean that. But however much I loved her, I've given you that love now as well.'

*   *   *

The first time Nick had invited a girl to the house, just for Sunday afternoon tea, Jake had been appalled. He had locked himself up in his room and refused to come down. Embarrassed, shocked at himself for causing Jake such distress, Nick had apologised and asked the girl to leave. Stupid of him, he had thought, stupid and insensitive. It was far too soon. In time, it would become easier . . .

When he went to try and talk to Jake, he was lying on the floor, gazing at the mural and the mermaid.

'Just leave me alone,' he said. 'Just go and talk to her if you want to.'

'I don't,' Nick said. 'She's gone.'

'Good.' But he went on staring at the mural. It was days before he so much as smiled.

*   *   *

'You'll have to be firm,' Trish, Nick's sister, said, when this had happened a couple more times. 'He can't stay joined at the hip with you for ever.'

'I don't think firmness is the answer,' said Nick with a sigh. 'God knows what it is.' Finding the right girl, he supposed. For both of them.

He had hoped so much that Julie was the right

64

girl.

He liked her too much to let her go. He continued to see her, lying to Jake about where he was, what he was doing, feeling like a guilty adolescent. Weeks went past; they met twice a week.

Their relationship moved on; he had stayed at her flat twice, had sent Jake to stay with Trish.

'I've got to go to a teachers' conference,' he said, blushing.

Trish laughed. 'Oh yes? Where is she holding it?'

'Don't tell Jake. It's too soon. He's so little. And so hurt.'

'He's not quite so little, Nick. He's nine years old.'

'I know. I know. But he is hurt.'

Jake knew his father was with Julie. He hated the idea so much it made him feel sick. Thinking of him doing the things they had always done together, with her. Like going to McDonald's and the cinema and walking in the park. As long as he wasn't mating with her . . . He knew about mating; they'd learnt about it at school. It sounded really weird; but he supposed, once you got used to the idea, it must be all right. His parents must have done it, after all, to get him. It was the whole point, he knew that, of mating. It made babies. Supposing Julie had a baby; that would be really awful.

She'd come to the house once or twice since the first time. Trying to make him like her. She'd bought him something he'd wanted for ages, a PlayStation 3 complete with an advanced Lego Batman game. He had thanked her for it with an icy politeness, because he knew he had to, but he never played with it, just put it at the bottom of his

65

underwear drawer.

'She's horrible,' he said to the mermaid. 'Horrible and stupid. Thinking she can make me like her just by giving me things. Why can't my dad see it?'

The mermaid on the rock looked back at him sadly, as she combed her hair. He was sure she understood.

*　　　*　　　*

Julie was worried about Jake. She loved Nick— enough to dream about marrying him. They got on so well, different as they were. Different as she was from Mary.

He was intrigued by the difference too.

'I can't believe it,' he said one night, 'that I can love someone like you.'

She had laughed.

'Am I so dreadful?'

'No. You're wonderful. But I thought high-powered people like you were tough and self-centred and out for all they could get.'

She laughed and kissed him.

'I am. I'm out to get you.'

'You've got me, Julie, you really have.'

But she knew she hadn't. Not really. Because of Jake.

*　　　*　　　*

He just wasn't going to let her win. She went on bringing him presents, offering treats, talking to him, teasing him, even ignoring him. It was quite hard, actually; there were times when he could feel

66

himself wanting to like her. Like when he didn't get in the swimming team and instead of telling him it didn't matter, she said it happened to her once and she'd hidden one of the other girls' swimsuits so she couldn't swim either. He thought that was really cool, although of course he hadn't said so. And when they went to the latest *Harry Potter* film and he was quite scared in some places and had shut his eyes, he knew she'd noticed and afterwards she said she'd been petrified and she couldn't understand why he wasn't too.

'She's just trying to get round me,' he said to the mermaid. 'Just trying to make me like her, so she can get round my dad. Well, she won't. I won't let her.'

The mermaid looked particularly sad that day.

Another time his father had bought him some poxy trainers from Marks & Spencer and she'd asked how he could even think of such a thing, and made him take them back and buy a Nike pair instead. That had been really difficult, not smiling and thanking her for them; but he'd managed. She'd left early, the evening after that happened; he could tell he'd upset her and his father as well. He felt a bit bad, but he went up to his room and stared very hard at the murals and the mermaid and thought about his mother. How could his father forget her like this? How could he?

*　　　*　　　*

Nick was taking Julie away to Paris for the weekend, for her birthday; it was all planned. Jake was going to stay with Trish and they were being taken to Chessington World of Adventures for the

67

whole of Saturday.

'He's just fine about it,' Nick said to Julie, giving her a kiss. 'He keeps saying how much he's looking forward to it.'

'Does he know where you're going?'

He looked awkward.

'Not exactly. I told him it was another conference.'

'Let's hope he doesn't find out,' she said, and her voice was heavy.

On the Friday evening, just as she was leaving the office, Nick rang her.

'I'm so sorry,' he said, 'Jake's really unwell. He says his throat hurts and he's just been sick. I can't leave him yet. Maybe we can go in the morning. I'll check with Eurostar.'

'Nick—'

'Julie, he can't help being ill.'

'Want to bet?' she said and slammed the phone down after telling him there was no way she was going in the morning.

He rang her back and they had a huge row, but she wouldn't give in.

Jake had been listening to this conversation from the top of the stairs; he scurried back to bed and lay back on his pillows as he heard his father's footsteps approaching. He had always been able to make himself sick to order. It was a very useful accomplishment. They must think he was really stupid. Who went to conferences at the weekend?

He looked at the mermaid. Somehow she didn't look as sweetly sympathetic as usual. Her green eyes were quite hard. He stuck his head under the bedclothes and pretended to be asleep.

68

Christmas was coming; Nick wanted more than anything to suggest that Julie spent it with them. He decided to talk to Jake first.

Jake didn't like the idea; not one bit.

'I don't know how you can even think of such a thing,' he said, and he meant it. 'Letting someone take Mum's place. For something as special as Christmas.'

'Jake, she wouldn't be taking Mum's place. She'd be taking her own. With us.'

'And what's that?' said Jake. He could hear his own voice, hostile and rude. 'What is her own place? She doesn't have one with us.'

'Yes she does. She's our friend. Friends should be together at Christmas.'

'She might be *your* friend,' said Jake. 'She isn't mine. And I don't want her to be. Least of all at Christmas.'

'Jake! Do you know what her present to you is?'

'No,' said Jake.

'It's tickets for *The Lion King*. For the three of us. Really, really good ones. You know how much you want to see that.'

'I don't want to see *The Lion King*. Not with her.'

His father looked at him very sadly for a while. Then he said, 'Jake, you're turning your back on a lot of happiness, you know. For me as well as you. It really isn't very sensible.'

'I don't care,' said Jake. 'Anyway, I don't like her. So how can I be happy with her?'

'Very easily. If you'll allow yourself.'

'Well, I won't,' said Jake, and ran upstairs to his room. He flung himself on the bed and started punching the pillow. Mixed with being pleased about Christmas, he felt cross with himself. He'd really wanted to see *The Lion King*.

He was careful not to look at the mermaid; he turned over and stared at the night-sky painting on the ceiling instead. It didn't look as brilliant and sparkly as usual.

*   *   *

Hearing that Jake didn't want to see *The Lion King* was the last straw for Julie. She really couldn't fight him any longer, however much she loved Nick: and she did love him. It was hopeless. There was no chance of their making any sort of life together. She spent Christmas with her mother, and told her everything; her mother said she'd take Jake over her knee and give him a good spanking.

'Oh, Mum. I don't know what good you think that would do.'

'Bring him to his senses. He's just a spoilt brat.'

'A very unhappy spoilt brat. He's still grieving for his mother.'

'Of course he is. But he's also having the time of his life, keeping his father all to himself. It's probably proving a very good distraction. Have you tried giving him a good talking to?'

'Mum! You don't understand. If I so much as breathe any criticism of Jake, Nick starts lecturing me.'

'Does he have to know?'

'Of course. He'd tell him.'

'And what about if you appealed to his better nature, explained how nice it would be for his father not to be alone all the time, that sort of thing?'

'He'd just say Nick wasn't alone, that he had him. And, anyway, he doesn't have a bad nature,' she added. She smiled at her mother; but it was a weak, watery smile.

*   *   *

Nick asked Trish if they could spend Christmas with her.

'Of course you can. But what about Julie? Wouldn't you rather be with her?'

'I would. Jake wouldn't.'

'Nick! You know what I think about—'

'Trish, he's still missing his mother. I can't force someone else on him.'

She sighed. 'All right. But it seems to me you're still going to be saying that when Jake's twenty-five.'

'Oh, don't be so ridiculous,' said Nick. But he looked very thoughtful as he put the phone down.

*   *   *

A job had come up at the New York office of Farquar and Fanshawe, and Julie had been told it was hers for the asking. She decided to ask for it.

She knew there was no point telling Nick the truth; he'd stop her somehow, keep on saying that it would be all right with Jake, that he'd come round in time, that she had to be patient. She'd had enough of being patient.

It didn't help that she wasn't feeling well. Sick and dizzy and desperately tired. Her mother guessed the reason; Julie looked at her in astonishment.

71

'Don't be ridiculous. It's . . . well, it's almost impossible.'

But she bought a pregnancy-testing kit and discovered it wasn't.

She got the job, as promised. Or nearly. Just a question, they said, of dotting i's and crossing t's. The New York office would like her to come over, meet the team and generally discuss terms. She said that would be fine. They booked her on a flight, business class, and into the New York Plaza Hotel. They were obviously very serious.

'What are you going to do?' said her mother.

'Take the job.'

'But what about the baby?'

She shrugged.

'They're giving me enough to pay two nannies. I'll manage. I won't tell them for a long time. I'll be fine.'

'You ought to tell Nick.'

'Yes, and he won't want it. Or Jake won't.'

'You don't know that.'

'Yes, I do.'

But she decided she would tell him anyway. She asked him to meet her after work.

'Come round to my flat, we can talk in peace there.'

Late that afternoon he phoned.

'I'm so sorry, Jake's not well. Really not well: temperature, horrible throat, the lot. No, Julie, this time it's genuine. We've seen the doctor. It's tonsillitis. I can't leave him. Can we give it a day or two?'

'No,' she said. 'Sorry, we can't.'

'Why not?'

'Because . . . because I'm going to New York. In

72

the morning. I've got a new job there—just going over to sign the contract.'

'Why didn't you tell me before?'

She was silent.

'Would you come round here, then?' he said. 'Please?'

*   *   *

Jake really felt ill. His throat was agony, and he felt sick. And he was so hot. He thought longingly of his mother, and how she had looked after him when he'd had tonsillitis. The best thing of all had been putting those bendy cooler packs from the freezer on his forehead and kind of round his neck. It had really helped. His father had said he couldn't find the bendy packs and put ice cubes in plastic bags instead, which hadn't done the same job at all.

His mother had also read to him for as long as he'd wanted. His father wasn't that good at reading. He did it rather as if he was teaching a class. Still, it was better than nothing. He'd bought the latest Harry Potter, which Jake hadn't read yet.

Only now he announced that *she* was coming round.

'Sorry, old chap. Not for long, but it's important. I'll read to you till she gets here, promise.'

'No, it's all right,' said Jake. He felt near to tears. This of all nights, and she'd be here, all shiny and noisy and bringing him something she thought he'd like. 'I'd rather go to sleep, I think.'

His father went downstairs; Jake looked at the mermaid and felt like crying.

'I want Mum so much,' he said. 'Not her, not even Dad. You understand, don't you?'

73

The mermaid looked sorrowfully back.

*   *   *

He heard Julie arrive; he heard them talking in the hall, heard his father say, 'No, he's half asleep already,' heard her footsteps on the stairs. She came in and looked at him. She didn't look so shiny; she was sort of huddled into a big thick coat he hadn't seen her wearing before, and she looked tired and had dark circles under her eyes and she was very pale.

'I've brought you something,' she said.

'I don't want anything.'

'You'll want this. It'll make you feel better.'

She suddenly sat down on the bed, closed her eyes.

'Are you all right?' he said. He was surprised that he cared.

'Yes. I'm fine. Just a bit—tired.'

'You've gone green,' he said.

'I'm all right. I feel a bit—sick.'

She pulled something out of her pocket, wrapped in newspaper.

'Here,' she said. 'One for your forehead, two for your throat. Let me put them on for you. I used to get sore throats and my mum said this would make me feel better. It really worked.'

She unwrapped three freezer packs.

Jake was too astonished to say thank you, and there was a sharp prickling behind his eyes. He shut them. He didn't want her to see he was almost crying. He couldn't say thank you.

'Well,' she said, after a bit. 'I'm going downstairs to talk to your father. Don't worry, it won't take long. Then you can have him back, all to yourself. For ever, probably.'

For some reason, he didn't like that 'for ever'. It sounded a bit . . . final. He looked at the mermaid: her expression seemed to be rather anxious, as she combed her hair.

*   *   *

He heard their voices downstairs in the sitting room, quiet at first, then getting noisier. He heard his father shouting that Julie was intolerant and insensitive and her shouting back that he was ridiculous and deluded. He heard his own name once or twice; after that, he put his head under the pillow. He didn't want to hear any words. Finally he heard the door open, heard them in the hall, heard Julie shouting, half crying.

'I'm going away,' she said, 'and I won't be back. I hope you'll be very happy together.'

'But I love you,' he heard his father say suddenly. 'I love you very, very much.'

'Not enough,' she said. 'Not nearly enough. Sorry. And don't even think about trying to stop me. I've had enough. And I'll tell you who I feel sorriest for. Not you; not me. That poor little mixed-up kid upstairs. So he loved his mother. Of course he did. She was obviously the most wonderful person—much more wonderful than me. But she's gone. He has to move forward. You both do. And I don't think you ever will. Goodbye, Nick.'

The door slammed; he heard her shiny car roaring away down the street, and then his father coming upstairs rather heavily. He opened the door and looked at Jake.

'I just thought you'd like to know,' he said, 'that we won't be seeing Julie any more. She's going to live in New York. In the morning, actually.'

'New York! That's a long way away.'

'Yes, well, I thought you'd like that.'

He looked awfully sad, Jake thought. Just for a moment, he felt sad too.

Then he said, 'Yes, I would like it. Of course. Dad, I'm really tired. I want to go to sleep now.'

Only he couldn't sleep. He lay there, thinking about what she had said about his mother being so wonderful—much more wonderful than her. It made her seem much nicer. And about how he and his dad had to move forward. He hadn't thought of it that way before. He looked at the mermaid.

'It wouldn't be forgetting Mum, would it?' he said. 'Not really. It would just be more . . . Well, doing things a bit differently.'

The mermaid looked back at him. Her eyes weren't hard as they had been the other day.

He put the light on, and went over to his drawer to get out a clean hanky, and saw the PlayStation tucked underneath his socks and T-shirts. He pulled it out and went back to bed. As he pulled his duvet up, he saw a scrumpled piece of paper lying there. It must have come out of her pocket with the ice packs. He straightened it out.

Pregnancy-Testing Kit, it read. *Instructions for Use*.

Jake felt quite dizzy himself. This must mean they had been mating. And she was having a baby. Obviously. She'd said she felt sick. People did feel sick when they were pregnant. He remembered his Aunt Trish being sick a lot before she had her baby. How horrible would that be! A baby in the house.

He'd never get any time with his father at all. It was a very good thing she was going to New York. His father never needed to know.

'She's having a baby,' he said to the mermaid. 'But she's going to New York. So that's all right, isn't it?'

Only, he felt a funny sort of lump in his throat that wasn't tonsillitis. And his eyes felt a bit funny too. Sort of stingy. He looked at the PlayStation and it was a bit blurry somehow. New York! That was a long way away. Well—it was really good. He was glad. He tucked away the PlayStation under the bedclothes so his father wouldn't see it if he looked in on him, and turned the light out again. It took him a very long time to go to sleep.

*   *   *

In the morning, he still felt terrible. He managed to wash and clean his teeth, but after that he felt really wobbly again. He went back to bed and stared up at the ceiling. He realised he actually still felt funny about Julie going away. Well, she'd been around for ages. He'd kind of got used to her. Didn't mean he liked her. Didn't mean he wanted her moving in or anything like that. And certainly not with a baby. He kept trying to tell himself how wonderful it was that she'd gone, but he didn't feel as happy as he'd thought he would. Perhaps she was right. Maybe they should move forward, him and his dad. Well, he'd know next time. He'd be nicer to the next one.

He kept thinking about Julie, about how kind she'd been to him—or tried to be, if only he'd let her—how she'd always known exactly which toys and books he'd like, how she talked to him as if he was a grown-up. He thought about refusing to go to *The Lion King* and how that hadn't really been very nice of him. And he thought about the other girls his father had brought home. They'd been awful, compared to Julie. They'd all talked to him as if he'd been about three.

'She was—nice,' he said suddenly. 'Nicer than I thought, anyway. I wish I'd been a bit nicer back.'

The mermaid stared sadly into her mirror.

*   *   *

Nick also woke up feeling terrible: as near to despairing as he could remember since Mary had died. And dreadfully alone again. He debated telephoning Julie—telling her he was sorry, asking her if they could try just once more—and decided there was no point. Nothing had changed; and Jake had to remain his first priority. He couldn't force someone on him that he didn't like.

*   *   *

Julie had got used to waking up feeling terrible, but today was worse than usual. Misery and remorse washed over her; had she been too harsh, too unforgiving with Jake? And was her mother right? Should she have told Nick about the baby? Was it worth just one more try? She had actually lifted the phone to dial Nick's number, but then she saw Jake's hard little face, staring at her in dislike, and heard Nick saying he must come first and put it down again. Nothing was going to change— whatever happened.

78

Jake was half asleep again when his dad came in; he looked very tired, Jake thought, and sort of grey. A bit like Julie had the night before.

'Sorry, old chap. I've got to go to school for a few hours. Inspectors are coming. Mrs Perkins is coming to sit with you. I'll be back about twelve.'

Mrs Perkins was their cleaner; Jake liked her.

'OK,' Jake said. And then, 'Dad?'

'Yes?'

'There's . . . I mean . . . are you sad about Julie going?'

'Yes, of course. But . . . Well, I don't think she's right for us. That's what you think too, isn't it?'

Jake didn't say anything. Then, in a rush, he managed it. 'Actually, I did quite like her. She wasn't too bad.'

'You didn't behave like you liked her.'

'Well . . .'

'Jake, you didn't. Anyway, it's too late now. She's had enough of both of us. I can't get her back.'

It didn't seem like he knew about the baby. Maybe Jake should tell him. Just so he knew . . .

Nick looked at his watch.

'Jake, I can't talk any more now. I'll be late. Mrs Perkins is downstairs. Hope you feel better soon.'

He looked at the mermaid when his father had gone. He felt terribly sad suddenly, and terribly guilty. He'd made both of them, his father and Julie, really miserable; and now he felt miserable too. He started to cry. Mrs Perkins came in and told him he mustn't upset himself and offered to read him a story. He shook his head. She left him, closing the door quietly behind her.

He couldn't stop crying.

'She was nice, really,' he kept whispering to the mermaid. 'I've changed my mind; I don't want her to go. I don't even mind her having a baby, not really. As long as it's a boy, anyway. I wish I could tell her.'

And he realised he couldn't and cried harder than ever.

*   *   *

Julie was sitting in the club-class lounge at the airport when her mobile rang. Funny; she'd been sure she'd turned it off. She checked it. She had. Must be the aircraft interfering with the system in some way. She put it in her bag and went back to her mineral water—oh, for a stiff gin and tonic— and the presentation she was going to make to the New York office when she got there. The phone rang again. This was weird. She looked at the number. It wasn't one she recognised.

'Julie?' It was a terrible line, very faint.

'Who's that? I can hardly hear you. Mum, is that you?' No one else would be ringing her now.

'Julie, Nick wants to talk to you. He's got something important to tell you. And he's really happy about the baby.'

'The baby! How on earth did he— Mum, you shouldn't have told him. That was very wrong of you.'

'Just ring him. Oh, and there's something else.'

The line went very crackly; Julie shook it.

'What?'

'Jake's been crying all morning. He doesn't want you to go. He really doesn't.'

80

'It's a bit late for that,' she said coolly. 'And, anyway, how do you know?'

'I've been with him. Give him a call, Julie. Please.'

The line went dead. She looked at the flight board. Her flight had just been called. She supposed she could just fit in a call . . . And found she suddenly felt rather happy.

*   *   *

Nick was sitting in his meeting; there was a dull leaden misery in his stomach. He kept hearing his sister's voice saying he couldn't go on like this and that Jake wasn't so little, and Julie's voice saying he had to move on. Were they right? Should he really stand up to Jake? Too late, though; she had gone; she'd be on a plane by now.

His mobile shrilled; everyone frowned at him. Funny; he'd been sure he'd switched it off.

'Sorry,' he said hastily and checked it. It was off. But it rang again.

'Sorry,' he mumbled, 'must be a fault. I'll put it outside.'

Outside he looked at the number; he didn't recognise it. But there was a message—to ring Julie. On her mobile.

'Julie?'

'Yes?'

'I got a message to call you.'

'A message? Not yet. But I was just going to ring you. Nick, Mum says—Mum says you're really happy about the baby.'

'The baby!'

'Yes. You are happy, aren't you, Nick? Please,

81

please say you are.'

'I . . .' He tried to stop the room swirling. 'The baby! Er . . . Your baby?'

'Well, of course. Our baby.'

Nick had once done a belly flop and had all the air knocked out of his stomach; he felt like that now: dizzy, a bit sick and absolutely confused.

'Our baby? Did you say, "our baby"?'

'Yes. Our baby. You are happy about it, aren't you?'

'Of . . . of course I am,' he said carefully. 'Of course.' And discovered he was. Very happy. Terribly, terribly happy. Or would be. When he got used to the idea . . .

'And also, she said that Jake's been crying all morning. Because I'm going. And he wants me to stay.'

'I . . . don't know, I'm afraid. I haven't been there.'

'Oh, I see. Well, she seemed quite sure. Anyway—listen—I don't have to go to New York. Well, I do now, but I can come right back again. If you want me to.'

'I want you to,' he said. 'So very much.'

'I will. I'm so happy. So terribly happy. I love you, Nick.'

'I love you too,' he said.

Julie phoned her mother.

'That was very naughty of you,' she said. 'Very naughty indeed. But I'm glad you did it.'

'Did what?' said her mother.

'Phoned Nick. Told him everything. I don't know what you're doing there, but—'

'Phoned Nick? Doing where? Julie, what is this? I'm at work, I haven't phoned anyone . . .'

'Oh, Mum! You're a terrible liar. Never mind. Thank you. And—it's so wonderful about Jake.'

'Jake!'

'Yes. Look, I must go. Final call. I'll ring you from New York. But I'm not taking that job.'

*　　　*　　　*

Nick drove home very fast and walked rather unsteadily upstairs. He went into Jake's room and looked at him. He looked much better; he was fast asleep, and his temperature was obviously down.

'He's been ever so upset, bless him,' said Mrs Perkins. 'Wouldn't tell me why. But he's calmed down now. And the sleep should do him good.'

'Mrs Perkins, has . . . has anyone else been here this morning?'

'No, of course not. Just me and Jake.'

'Nobody at all? Are you sure?'

'Well, put it this way,' said Mrs Perkins, 'I think I'd have noticed if they had been.'

'And you didn't make a phone call to me? At the school?'

'No. No, of course not. You said only if Jake was really much worse.' She looked anxious. 'Should I have done?'

'No, of course not,' said Nick.

He sat down on Jake's bed and looked at him. He was holding the PlayStation in his hand, and three ice packs were piled up neatly on the bedside table. Nick looked across at the mural—the mural that Mary had painted with such love. The one Jake liked best; the one with the mermaid.

He looked at the mermaid; she was sitting there, on the rock, combing her hair, her tail shimmering

83

in the water. And just for a moment, he could have sworn that instead of a mirror she had a mobile phone in her hand.

Just a trick of the light. Of course.

KNOWING BEST

Laura Maddox and Fergus O'Connell were very fond of telling people they had met at an old people's home. Since they were both young, stylish and successful, it was not a story that was very easy to believe; nevertheless, it was perfectly true in essence, if not in detail, and was made much of in the speeches at their wedding.

The detail was that the meeting place had been not quite an old people's home, rather a very expensive nursing home, where Laura's widowed grandmother was recovering from a hip operation and complaining ceaselessly about having to live with a lot of old people (most of whom were in fact the same age as, if not a little younger than, herself), and Fergus's twice-divorced great-uncle, in a room just two along the corridor, was recovering from a very nasty bout of pneumonia and was constantly in trouble with the nurses for locking himself in the lavatory with a flask of his best Irish whiskey.

But it made a good story, and Laura's grandmother, whose name was Lucinda (Mrs Beresford, the Hon.), and Fergus's great-uncle, whose name was Edmund (christened Eeamonn, but changed in a bid for respectability during his early years at the Bar), were guests of honour at the wedding. They were observed dancing the Charleston rather energetically during its closing stages, when most of the younger guests had succumbed to the joint rigours of alcohol and stress-induced exhaustion, and Fergus and Laura did wonder if a second wedding might ensue, but it was not to be. Lucinda told Laura that Edmund might be as charming and handsome as his great-nephew, indeed even more so in her view, but he was not good husband material. 'One divorce I could overlook, darling, two—rather more serious.' And Edmund told Fergus that, while Laura's grandmother was beautiful and fascinating, as indeed was her granddaughter, she was undoubtedly a woman with a strong mind of her own and, at his stage in life, he needed someone with a sweetly pliable one. But they remained great friends and met for lunch at least once a month at the Connaught Hotel, where the first thing they discussed (over the Bellinis they both adored) was the progress of the Maddox–O'Connell marriage.

At first, the progress was good: the honeymoon (in the Seychelles) had been marvellous; the small house acquired in Fulham, delightful; Laura's job with the premier-league London solicitors, Buchman Hardacre, fantastic; Fergus's, with the London property company, Welling Wright Wolfe, amazing. Lucinda and Edmund were invited to a Christmas drinks party at the Fulham house and, over lunch the next day, agreed that Laura and Fergus were perfectly suited.

'She's made a man of him,' said Edmund, 'not just a charming boy. Another Bellini?'

'He lights her up,' said Lucinda. 'He's brought her out, made her sparkle. Yes, please. As it's

Christmas.'

*　　　*　　　*

Laura and Fergus had a very happy Christmas, although Laura had found it a little trying when Fergus had been late for their own party. Had it really been necessary to take a client to a wine bar at five that afternoon? And his habit of flirting with just about everyone was beginning to get on her nerves. And when he didn't get home in time to trim the tree with her on the night before Christmas Eve, it was almost the last straw.

But she forgave him everything on Christmas morning, when he appeared in a red dressing gown with a tray of champagne and orange juice and a big stocking filled with presents just for her, endless jokey things that he had spent time and trouble finding. And finally, right at the bottom, The Present: wrapped in the wonderfully recognisable blue box with the white satin ribbon, a Tiffany gold coffee bean on a chain.

'Oh, Fergus, it's beautiful. So special. I've wanted one for ages. How did you know? I've never mentioned it, ever.'

'Call it male intuition,' he said, leaning forward and kissing her. And then one thing led to another and the red dressing gown came off (as did her white one), the presents cascaded on to the floor and Christmas lunch (which they had agreed they should spend alone) was very late indeed.

After Christmas, things became a little less happy. Lucinda reported to Edmund that Laura was looking very tired and a bit tense. 'Fergus's company had to make some redundancies and he

86

was one of the first to go. He's got another job, but it doesn't pay so well. And now he's started playing poker, of all things, with some of his colleagues, and he's out one or two nights a week. It doesn't sound good to me.'

Edmund said it sounded fine to him, and that the boy was only trying to make his way in the world and have a bit of fun; but he invited Fergus out for a meal one night at his club and probed a bit.

Fergus wolfed down an enormous meal of beef Wellington followed by treacle pudding. 'What a treat! Laura would have a fit if she could see me. She doesn't approve of this sort of thing, you know.'

He liked the new job, he said. It was less pressurised than the last one, and money wasn't everything, after all. And with Laura earning twice what he did, anyway, it didn't really matter too much. Edmund did suggest that one night a week was more than enough for the poker games, but reported to Lucinda that, otherwise, things seemed more or less all right.

'It's difficult for a young man with a wife more successful than he is. And, call me old fashioned, but I do think he needs a square meal when he gets home.'

Lucinda said she would call him very old fashioned, but there was nothing necessarily wrong with that and, the next time she saw Laura, she did remark casually that she thought Fergus was looking rather thin and maybe needed more than a small plate of pasta for his dinner, working as hard as he did.

'You'll be telling me the way to a man's heart is through his stomach, next,' Laura said irritably, adding that she certainly didn't have the time

87

to start cooking meat and two veg when she got in from work, and that she was the major breadwinner. Lucinda said that Fergus might be finding that a little hard to cope with and Laura said that he was finding it rather easy, as far as she could see, and she parted with her grandmother rather coolly.

*   *   *

Laura found marriage increasingly difficult as that second year wore on. For a start, wherever they went and whatever they were doing, Fergus was late. He had always been late, of course—it was in his nature, part of him, as much as his lop-sided smile and his wild hair and his way of running his hands through it when he was about to launch into an implausible explanation—but that was hardly an excuse, and it certainly didn't make her feel any better as she waited in empty cinema foyers, or tried to look interested in her phone over an empty glass in a wine bar, or chatted brightly at parties while watching the door edgily for his arrival. Then there was his way of leaving her little notes, telling her he loved her, in unexpected places like the top of the laundry basket or the cereal packet. Against her will, Laura found herself thinking that she would actually welcome finding the laundry basket taken downstairs and emptied into the washing machine, or finding the cereal packet cleared away along with the breakfast bowls, rather than the notes. She tried to tell herself it was unreasonable and unromantic of her, but it didn't quite work.

The fact that the kitchen cupboards that he had promised to install were still in their flatpacks quite annoyed her, too; as did the way the garden had become a showplace for rare British weeds. And then there was an increasing lack of ambition, which she found it hard to come to terms with, and the flirting with every pretty woman he ever met was harder still. She would sit, pretending to ignore it, as it went on at the other side of the dinner table or the dance floor, feeling stiff and wretched herself, not responding to whatever anyone might be saying to her, while girls giggled and whispered and fluttered their eyelashes at Fergus and he smiled and teased and flattered them back.

*   *   *

They began to have rows about it; she would become tense and miserable if they were going out, would warn him in the car on the way, trying to sound light hearted, not to do it to her, that it was boring and irritating. At first he would laugh and try to tease her about it and then he became irritated himself and proceeded to flirt harder than ever. Of course, it was only flirting; he would never actually cheat on her, never have an affair; she was quite, quite sure of that. 'I know he loves me,' she said fretfully to Lucinda, 'and I do love him. We just seem to be . . . well, drifting apart a bit. So busy, both of us, that's the trouble. And his company's started sending him out of town at least once a week. It doesn't help.'

Lucinda said that of course it didn't and suggested that Laura worked a little less hard herself. 'Money isn't everything, darling.' After Laura had gone, she wrote Fergus a note, asking him in for a drink one evening, as she needed his advice on a property that she owned. With the advice given and two of her very generous gin and tonics down Fergus's throat, she told him gently and very sweetly that she thought he should perhaps work a little less hard for a while, and spend more time at home with Laura. 'She needs you more than perhaps you realise. Of course, I'm just a silly old woman but I'm very fond of you, and I know you can make her happy.'

Fergus kissed her and told her she was neither old nor silly and that he would try to make sure that the evenings working away from home stopped immediately. 'It's difficult, you know, marriage, sometimes.'

Lucinda patted his hand and said she did indeed know, and that she had occasionally had to leave her own husband for the odd few days to visit her sisters or friends. 'He was a bit—quiet, and of course getting away did cheer me up, but in the end I found it less unsettling to stay at home.'

*   *   *

That Christmas, the Tiffany box in Laura's stocking contained an eternity ring. Her new year's resolution, she told Fergus, was to cook a proper meal at least twice a week. Early in February, Fergus took Edmund out to lunch and told him he was to become a great-great-uncle. 'We are both so happy. We've had a few ups and downs, but this is a new beginning. Isn't it marvellous?'

Edmund said it was indeed marvellous and ordered a bottle of Bollinger, adding over the second or maybe the third glass that he hoped Fergus would be mindful that women in Laura's condition needed a lot of cosseting, 'and can be quite demanding from time to time, as I recall.' Fergus said he would be mindful and indeed he was and even began putting away the cereal packets and loading up the washing machine and looking for another, better paid, job so that Laura would be able to give up work; she could never remember being so happy.

*   *   *

Later that year, in June, Fergus was driving them down a winding country lane with perhaps not quite enough care and attention. He was singing along with Britney Spears and hit a car coming in the other direction; nobody was seriously hurt, but Laura got a nasty blow on the head and was very shocked; twenty-four hours later, she lost the baby.

*   *   *

She was horribly depressed afterwards: depressed and withdrawn from Fergus. He just didn't understand how she felt. 'I feel so angry with him. And he keeps saying we can have another, as if the baby was a car or something that could be replaced.'

'Men can't understand these things,' said Lucinda, adding carefully, 'but don't shut him right out, darling. He wants to help.'

Laura continued to shut Fergus out; he was patient with her for a long time, but when, after three months, he was still not allowed near her, physically or emotionally, he became depressed and demoralised himself.

'She won't let me even try to comfort her,' he said to Edmund. 'I feel so useless, such an absolute failure. I'm in despair.'

*   *   *

By late November, Fergus was working away from London at least once a week; there was no Tiffany box that Christmas and, in February, he told Edmund that Laura wanted a divorce.

'I was . . . fooling around with someone,' he said, helping himself to a tumbler of Edmund's whiskey. 'Bloody stupid, I know, but Laura was . . . well, let's say you'd have thought she wouldn't care—from her behaviour. Oh, God. And I love her so much. What would you do, if you were me?'

Edmund said he had been there once or twice himself, and didn't know of anything that could be done. Lucinda, holding Laura in her arms while she wept and railed, felt much the same.

The solicitors got to work.

*   *   *

Halfway through that year, Laura met Michael. Michael was everything Fergus was not. He was never late; he never flirted with anyone; he was a lawyer, like her—extremely hard working and ambitious—and he also did things like making dinner and fixing things when they broke. He was not exactly good-looking, Laura told Lucinda, 'But he always looks . . . well, nice. And he's not especially amusing or anything, but he listens to what I say and takes notice of it. And he wants to meet you. I know you'll love him.'

92

Lucinda thought Michael was awful. 'Dull as ditchwater,' she said to Edmund. 'No sense of humour and he wears his virtue horribly visibly. Keeps telling Laura he's been to the supermarket for her and taken the curtains to the dry cleaners. Won't do her any good at all.'

'He makes me really happy. You do like him, don't you?' Laura said to Lucinda.

Lucinda said carefully that she thought Michael seemed very nice, but of course she didn't really know him yet.

Laura looked at her. 'I know you had a soft spot for Fergus,' she said. 'A very soft one. But you didn't have to live with him. And . . . and share him. I need someone like Michael. Someone reliable and . . . and safe.'

'She doesn't, of course,' said Lucinda to Edmund. 'She just thinks she does. Fergus has hurt her very badly, but she still loves him. In my opinion.'

Edmund reported this back to Fergus, who looked at him gloomily. 'Maybe it won't last,' he said without the slightest conviction.

'I understand he's moving in. Complete with a set of recipe books and his own iron.'

'Silly bastard!' said Fergus, vehemently.

'You still in love with Laura, are you, then?'

'Terribly,' said Fergus. 'I don't know how I could have been such a fool.'

'You should tell her.'

'I've tried—over and over again. She won't listen. And why should she?'

Edmund felt bound to agree, but reported back to Lucinda, anyway.

'He's dreadfully sorry. Filled with remorse.'

93

'Remorse comes cheap,' said Lucinda briskly. 'He's behaved very badly.'

'With no cause whatsoever, would you say?'

'Well—almost no cause.'

Edmund nodded, then he said, 'They're both very young. Young and foolish. They don't really know what's good for them.'

Lucinda agreed; the unspoken rider to this being that they did and that Laura and Fergus were good for one another.

The divorce machinery ground on; Laura, quietly determined, refused to discuss matters with Fergus. Michael had finished all the kitchen cupboards, planted over a hundred bulbs for the spring and been made a partner. Fergus was living in solitary squalor in a flat in Hammersmith.

*　　　*　　　*

He met Charlotte at a party. Charlotte had her own property company: she was tough, glamorous and very ambitious. And looking for someone just like Fergus.

'It's awfully good,' Fergus said to Edmund, 'to be with someone who seems to fancy me occasionally.'

This was an understatement; Charlotte made it plain she could not get enough of him. Within weeks they were an item. Fergus asked Edmund if he might bring her to supper one night. 'I'd like to know what you think of her. She's very different from Laura.'

*　　　*　　　*

'She's dreadful,' said Edmund to Lucinda, 'hard as

nails and talking already as if she owns the boy—
telling him he's got to get a better job, saying he's
not fulfilling his potential. Criticising his friends,
making him give up the poker games. He's looking
hen-pecked already.'

'Oh dear,' said Lucinda, adding, 'Laura's
changed too. Getting rather—smug. And wearing
some really rather dull clothes. I'm glad she's
happy, but . . .'

*   *   *

The divorce would become final early in the new
year. Just before Christmas, Laura went to see
Lucinda. She looked different: more how she used
to look.

'I . . . saw Fergus last night,' she said.

'Fergus!'

'Yes. We met at some do in London. Michael
wasn't invited and Fergus was so late, his new
woman left in a temper.' Her lips twitched. 'I
should have done that, I suppose. Instead of
complaining.'

'Much better idea,' said Lucinda.

'He . . . suggested we have dinner. What do you
think? I mean—I'd like us to be friends again.'

Lucinda, choosing her words carefully, said
it sounded very sensible to her, 'but what would
Michael say about it?'

'Oh—he's away for a few days, painting his
mother's kitchen. He's so wonderful,' she added
quickly.

'He is indeed,' said Lucinda.

'She looked wonderful,' she said to Edmund.

'So did the boy. Marvellous.'

95

It was all fairly inevitable, really. Dinner went on for five hours. Moving from awkwardness over the starters, to remorse and then reminiscence over the main course, and flirtation over the dessert.

Over a final glass of champagne, Laura found herself holding Fergus's hand; in the taxi, Fergus began to kiss her; somehow he never went home.

*   *   *

'This is terrible,' wailed Laura, waking to find him sitting on the bed with a tray of champagne and orange juice.

'It's wonderful,' said Fergus. 'All night was wonderful. And I love you. So very much. Still.'

'I love you too. Still.'

*   *   *

Laura told Michael; he was sanctimoniously reproachful. 'You'll regret it—again. He won't change. People don't.'

*   *   *

Fergus decided to tell Charlotte over dinner. He knew she'd be angry; the prospect made him nervous. He decided that he would, under the circumstances, give her her Christmas present. It would soften the blow—she was that sort of girl. And, besides . . . Well, you never quite knew. She'd told him exactly what she wanted and, although it

had given him a bit of a nasty moment, he'd bought it. It was a small gold coffee bean on a chain. From Tiffany's . . .

Before going to meet her, he put it in his pocket. He'd written a card. *Thank you for everything*, it said.

But he got her wrong. Having heard what he had to say, she threw the box back at him, unopened, with a few clearly delivered home truths—including the observation that Laura must be even more of a fool than she'd thought, 'taking a layabout like you back.'

*   *   *

Fergus phoned Laura; he was missing her. Could he come round?

Laura said he could. Several very happy hours ensued.

*   *   *

Fergus was in the shower when Laura found the Tiffany box with the label saying, *Thank you for everything*. She rather tremulously opened it and discovered it could not possibly be intended for her.

*   *   *

'There's no point my trying to explain,' he said, standing, white faced, while she shouted at him. 'You won't believe me and you won't listen.'

*   *   *

'The boy's made a complete ass of himself,' said Edmund on the phone to Lucinda, 'and this time I really can't see how he's going to get out of it.'

*   *   *

'And to think I believed him,' Laura said to Lucinda, her face ravaged with tears. 'All those things he said about how sorry he was, how he would never do it again. To think he'd do . . . that.'

'What, darling? What did he do?'

'Only bought her the same Christmas present he once bought me. He's obviously still seeing her; it was in his pocket. The bastard! The absolute bastard. God, I should have listened to Michael. And now—'

Lucinda passed her her handkerchief.

'My darling,' she said, 'you really shouldn't leap to conclusions. It's a terrible fault of yours. Now, stop crying and listen to me.'

*   *   *

Later that afternoon, Fergus was working at his desk when the door opened and Laura walked in. Her eyes were very large and very soft.

'Why didn't you tell me?' she said.

'Tell you what?' he said, his expression carefully puzzled.

'About the necklace. That it was for Grandmother. I would have believed you. Of course I would.'

Fergus pushed his hands through his hair. Then he smiled at her.

'I don't know that you would,' he said, 'actually.

98

But let's just say I'm glad she told you.'

At the Connaught Hotel, Lucinda and Edmund toasted the reunion.

'What a good day's work,' said Lucinda, just slightly smug.

'Indeed.' He was silent. Then, 'I hope we have done the right thing.'

'Of course we have,' said Lucinda. She was silent too. Then, 'Haven't we?' she added, just slightly less certainly.

GLASS SLIPPER

Autumn 1994

Cinderella case jury out. Verdict expected this afternoon.

Eleanor Coleman looked at the newspaper placards, and then at the man sitting beside her in the taxi. He managed a rather weak smile.

'I feel sick,' he said. 'How about you?'

'A bit,' she said. 'I know it's still very much in the balance. But either way, we've done well. The general public certainly thinks you should be the winner. So . . .'

'The general public aren't going to pay me damages. Or costs.'

'No, but you've had some brilliant publicity,' said Eleanor briskly. 'You'll get more work than you can ever handle in the future. And everyone's singing the wretched song. It's at number one again this week. So if we do win . . .'

'Yes, I know. Money coming out of our ears.

You've been marvellous, Eleanor. Absolutely marvellous. I still don't know quite why you decided to take the case on. When it looked so absolutely hopeless.'

'I might tell you one day,' said Eleanor. 'God, I hope this traffic clears. It's almost two thirty. We can't be late for the judge.'

They stopped outside the law courts at 2.25 p.m. Eleanor paid off the cab. The driver waved at her and grinned, gave her the thumbs-up sign. 'You're the solicitor in this Cinderella case, aren't you?' he said. 'Hope you win. Show the bastard where he gets off. You can tell he's a cheat, just by looking at him.'

'Well, we shall have to see,' said Eleanor, smiling at him sweetly. 'But thank you for your good wishes anyway.'

She walked rather slowly into the law courts, and stood waiting for her client, who was making what she hoped was a suitably non-committal statement to the hordes of press at his heels. Some of the things he'd said recently had been a little over the top. He looked very drawn, very tired. Poor man. And then, coming down the corridor towards her in the opposite direction, looking neither drawn nor tired but outrageously confident and cheerful, she saw him. Smiling at her, his dark eyes moving over her face, lingering on her mouth; and the years rolled away and she was nineteen years old again, dressed in layers of white and pink lace, her hair an expensive tangle of dark curls, the undoubted belle of the ball and ready to fall helplessly in love with anyone who came her way; and to live out her own version of the Cinderella story.

100

Spring 1977

'But I don't want to go the ball,' wailed Nell. 'I hate balls, you know I do. I hate all that stuff.'

'Darling, just to please your old godmother. I want to have a few more young people there; it would help me so much. Charles Drummond-Browne will be there,' she added.

'But . . .' Nell hesitated, looked at her godmother. She was terribly fond of her; she hated upsetting her. But she knew exactly what this ball would be like, full of old people like her godmother, who must be at least fifty now. How could people of that age even think of dancing? There was something faintly obscene about it. She did like Charles very much, though; he was so good-looking and clever—and extremely rich. Not that she cared about that, of course, but . . .

'Go on, Eleanor,' said Ursula with an encouraging smile, sensing her weakening. 'I'll buy you a new dress. And pay for you to have your hair done.'

That really was irresistible. Nell's die-straight brown hair was the bane of her life. 'Oh—all right.'

'Darling, thank you. I'll meet you at Harvey Nicks this afternoon. Two o'clock, side entrance.'

*   *   *

She arrived late at the ball because her hair went wrong, and then she couldn't get a taxi; she rushed over to Ursula's table, breathless and apologetic, just as everyone was about to start dinner. Charles, clearly torn between disapproval of her lateness and pleasure that she had finally arrived, stood up,

101

smiling with his careful charm. 'Better late than never,' he said. 'Come and have some champagne.'

It was a very good evening; she danced and talked with Charles most of the time. She had known him for a couple of months, had spent a few slightly formal but very pleasant evenings with him, and was more than half convinced that she was in love with him. He treated her with a rather old-fashioned courtesy, had kissed her fairly expertly and seemed to expect no more than that, which made a pleasant change. Most of the young men she knew assumed she was dying to get into bed with them in return for a pizza and a glass of cheap red wine. He was fifteen years older than she was, heir to a very old English baronetcy; he was also a highly successful barrister. Nell's mother, who was a rather hard-up widow, was extremely excited at the prospect of the romance.

'You look lovely,' said Charles, smiling down at her as they waltzed slightly formally round the floor. 'But then you always do.'

'Thank you,' said Nell.

'I'd—well, I'd like to see a lot more of you, Nell. Would you like that?'

'Yes,' she said, smiling up at him, her heart leaping pleasantly. 'Yes, Charles, I would.'

He pulled her closer. 'I'm a bit—well, old-fashioned, I know. I like to take things slowly. But I do think about you a great deal. And look forward to seeing you. How about you?'

Nell looked up at him, touched by his awkwardness, wanting to ease it.

'I feel just the same,' she said. She did. It wasn't rapture exactly, but it was very nice.

'Good,' he said. 'Then we must proceed, take

things further.'

She wondered, even in the midst of her pleasure, if that was how he talked to his clients in chambers.

*   *   *

They were sitting at the table, smiling slightly foolishly at one another, when the cabaret was announced.

'Christ,' groaned Charles. 'A chanteuse, I suppose.'

But it wasn't a chanteuse; it was an extraordinarily handsome young man, in white tie and tails, his dark hair slicked back, who played the piano and sang thirties numbers with great charm. After an initial repertoire, he said he would take requests.

There were a lot of predictable ones, like 'Tea for Two' and 'Top Hat', and then Nell stood up and asked for 'Dancing on the Ceiling'. He looked at her blankly for a moment, then smiled and began to play. He was really very accomplished. After about three more numbers, he played 'Dance, Little Lady' as an encore, and then came over to Nell's table, smiling.

'Well done,' he said. 'You almost had me there. Can I claim a dance as my prize?'

'Oh—yes,' said Nell, looking anxiously at Charles, who nodded just slightly coolly first at her, then the young man. 'Yes, thank you.'

He danced very well; Nell promptly felt she had not two but three left feet.

'Relax,' he said, and then, as the music changed, 'Here's a slow one. Let's talk. What's your name?'

'It's Eleanor,' said Nell, 'but everyone calls me

Nell.'

'I shall call you Ella. As in Cinderella. So appropriate for the belle of the ball. Which you certainly are. I hope you won't vanish at midnight.'

'I promise I won't,' said Nell. 'And you are?'

'Nick. Nick Buitoni. You could call me Buttons, I suppose. As I'm here strictly in a below-stairs capacity—I'm sure I'm not meant to dance with the guests.'

'Well I'm glad you did,' said Nell, and meant it.

'That's a peach of a dress.'

'Thank you.'

'And those earrings are wonderful. Pure deco. Where did you get them?'

'Jumble sale,' said Nell. 'Pure paste, I'm sure.'

'They suit you. Is that your boyfriend, watching us like a rather disapproving hawk?'

'Oh—yes. Yes, it is,' said Nell. For some reason she felt less happy at the idea than she had ten minutes earlier.

Suddenly he stopped dancing, took her face in his hands and kissed her gently on the mouth.

'You're lovely,' he said.

The most extraordinary sensation ripped through Nell: a piercing sweetness, half pleasure, half almost pain. She closed her eyes, kissed him back, just briefly, then pulled away, staring at him, shocked, shaken. Out of the corner of her eye she saw Charles, frozen-faced, calling her over, slightly imperiously.

'I'd better go,' she said to Nick Buitoni, her voice sounding strange even to herself. 'I am supposed to be with him.'

'Of course,' he said. 'Goodbye, Cinderella. I hope we'll meet again.'

It wasn't until she was in the ladies' much later on that she realised she had dropped one of her earrings.

*   *   *

Eleanor became Mrs Charles Drummond-Browne a year later in a lavish ceremony at St Margaret's, Westminster; the reception for seven hundred people (paid for at her charming insistence by her new mother-in-law) took place at Claridges, and the newly-weds spent a fortnight at the Drummond-Brownes' shooting lodge in Scotland before Charles had to return to chambers. The honeymoon was chilly in more ways than one. Charles as a lover was dutiful and competent rather than inspired. More than once, to her horror, Nell found herself thinking of Nick Buitoni and the sweet, probing warmth that had flooded through her when he kissed her at the ball, and wondered if she would ever know it again.

Nevertheless, when they returned to London she was pregnant with Flora, and two years after that, she presented Charles with the Honourable James Drummond-Browne, the heir to his title and estates. By then, she was fairly unhappy.

1981

'We have to go to the Red Cross ball,' said Charles. 'I know it's a bore, but old Geoffrey Blagdon asked if we'd join his table and I couldn't say no. Three weeks from tomorrow I think he said. Is that all right?'

'Well yes, I suppose so,' said Nell. 'And anyway,

what if it wasn't?'

'Oh for heaven's sake, darling, don't start that. I was just trying to sound considerate.'

'How kind.'

'And this time do you think you could make a huge effort to actually talk to Molly Blagdon, rather than just sitting there staring at your plate? It's highly embarrassing.'

'Charles, what am I supposed to say to her? She treats me like some kind of moronic child.'

'Maybe that's because you appear to her like a moronic child. I don't know, Nell. If you haven't worked out some dinner-table conversation by now, there seems very little hope of it ever happening.'

'Thanks,' said Nell, getting up from the table so that he wouldn't see the easy tears rising behind her eyes, and wondering where the breezy, self-confident person who had walked down the aisle to marry Charles had gone.

*   *   *

'Ah, Eleanor, you're sitting next to me. How nice. Come and tell me what you've been doing. You're looking a bit peaky, my dear; doesn't young Charles look after you properly?'

That just summed it up, thought Nell. He didn't look after her in any way at all; not emotionally, not physically, not intellectually. He treated her increasingly like some kind of rather irksome responsibility—even in bed. Most of all in bed. She couldn't actually remember when she had last enjoyed sex.

She smiled determinedly at Geoffrey Blagdon. 'Yes, of course he does. But the weather's been so beastly lately, I've hardly been out. You look wonderful,' she added carefully.

'Well, thank you, my dear. Don't often get a compliment from a pretty girl. Promise me the first dance, won't you?'

'Yes, of course,' said Nell.

'I don't believe it,' said a voice. That voice. That lovely, sexy, warm voice. 'Cinderella. Back at the ball. You did vanish that night. I came looking for you and I couldn't find you.'

Nell sat frozen to her chair, afraid even to turn round at first in case he was a hallucination, so often had she imagined this moment. Then she did turn, slowly, looked up, and there he was, a little older, but just as handsome, just as vividly, dangerously attractive.

'Hello,' was all she managed to say.

'You're a lot thinner. Marriage doesn't seem to agree with you. I read about it in the papers, your grand wedding to your Prince Charming. Are you all right?'

'Yes, of course,' she said, illogically indignant. 'And you?'

'Oh, I'm fine. Still struggling. Not played the Palladium yet. Look, I have something of yours. Here. I never go anywhere without it, just in case I find you. Now, I wonder. If it fits, I shall know . . .'

'Know what, if what fits?' said Nell, laughing, and then stared incredulously as Nick Buitoni produced from his pocket, wrapped carefully in a slightly yellowing silk handkerchief, a dangly paste earring.

'You dropped it when you fled. Here, put it on.'

'I can't,' said Nell, laughing. 'I'm wearing my mother-in-law's diamonds. Charles wouldn't like it.'

'Charles isn't going to get it,' said Nick Buitoni

lightly. 'Well, take it anyway. And come and dance with me. I seem to remember Cinderella and Buttons had a high old time of it in the kitchen.'

'Better than she had with the prince, probably,' said Nell with a sigh.

'You sound sad,' said Nick. 'Come along and tell me about it.'

Nell looked round; Charles was talking what was clearly business at another table. He wouldn't notice. And if he did, he wouldn't care. She stood up, took Nick's hand. A charge went through her, the same sweet warmth she remembered, still, after all these years. She followed him on to the floor and decided that fate could take matters over.

*　　　*　　　*

Fate propelled her into love: wild, tender, shaking, laughing, crying love. Nick Buitoni persuaded her into bed after a series of very long, seductive lunches, bombarding her with the full force of his considerable sexuality. Trying to analyse it afterwards, the nearest Nell came to describing that sexuality was that it was as cerebral as it was physical; he talked her into desire, used words, images, ideas that left her as weak and helpless against him as his mouth on hers, his hands moving over her, his body leading her to places and pleasures she had never even dreamed of. He had a studio flat in Highgate: a classically untidy bachelor place, with virtually no furniture except a huge bed, a low table, some big cushions, an old, distinctly honky-tonk piano and a superbly equipped kitchen, part of the main room, where he cooked small, exquisite delicacies for eating after love, washed

108

down with champagne brought by Nell. He played music, wonderful music, 'music to love to', he said: Mahler, Bach, Puccini, and sometimes the thirties tunes they both loved. Nell came alive in that room, learnt what happiness meant. She felt she was owed it; there was no guilt, just a sense of rightness. Nick had no other girlfriends, he said; he had just finished with someone, 'and then I went back to waiting for you'.

He earned the little money he had playing the piano and singing in nightclubs, and places like the Savoy, so he was always free for her in the day: 'You see, Ella, my darling, our lives are made for each other. We can live in the kitchen just like Buttons and his Cinders.'

* * *

The intrigue and deceit excited her, didn't really make her feel bad at all. It was easy to invent stories about her long absences at lunchtime; she was heavily involved in charity work, and one more committee meeting every week or so was hardly going to excite suspicion. They evolved a code: she would ring his number at work, and if he was out, she would say that Mrs Green at the Ealing number had called, could he ring her; nothing could be further from Lady Drummond-Browne of Chester Square, SW1, and Marley Park, Somerset, than Mrs Green from Ealing. And he would announce himself to her (or the nanny or the housekeeper) in a thin South London drawl as Brian Summers, or in a rich West Country roll as Dick Lacey. They invented lifestyles for Brian, who was an accountant's clerk working on one of her charities, and for Dick, who was a designer working on brochures for the many events she helped organise. It all added to the fun. Sometimes she rang him in the evening when she knew he was working, just to hear his voice. It sounded so exactly like him, that voice, she could see him at once, vividly, his handsome face, the dark brown eyes (so different from Charles's icy blue), the wild black hair, the ridiculously perfect teeth, the tall, rangy body (so unlike Charles's ramrod-straight one), and she would listen smiling to the silly message: 'You have reached the answering machine of Nick Buitoni. I am out on a doubtless abortive mission to obtain work on stage, screen or the airwaves. Please leave your name and number and I'll get back to you. Callers from Hollywood should contact my agent. Thanks for ringing.'

One day when she arrived, he was sitting at the piano, picking out a tune; it was haunting, sweet and swinging at the same time. Ella went over to him and kissed him, and he pulled her on to his knee.

'Like this?' he said. 'I wrote it for you. It's called "Cinderella". You can help me with the lyrics. What do you think? Listen . . .' He began to sing: '*Clock strikes, Midnight, Love is gone, Clock strikes, First light, Sad sweet song . . .*'

'It's terrible,' said Nell, laughing, 'but the music is lovely. Did you really write it?'

'Of course,' he said, his face hurt. 'What do you think I am, a rip-off artist?'

'You might be.'

'In that case, Cinders, I'm going to do some serious ripping off. Starting with that extremely expensive-looking sweater.'

110

She could never imagine afterwards how she had endured it for so long, almost two years, the half-and-half life: the one fairy story, fantasy, the other real, the one so filled with love, the other so empty of it, the one so joyful, the other so bleak; how she had reconciled guilt and pleasure, hope and fear, how adept she had become at lying, pretending, at building elaborate deceits. She considered quite often giving him up, and rejected it, afraid before it had even begun of the pain, the emptiness, the sheer awfulness of life without him. And she also waited, half hopefully, half fearfully, for him to move things on, make them better; dreamed, longed for his voice telling her he wanted her to leave Charles, to marry him. Only it never came; and she was too much of a coward to work out why.

Meanwhile Charles became richer and more successful, and colder and more critical, and Flora and James began to grow up. She tried and failed to persuade Charles that she should take up some kind of career; weathered the deaths of her mother and godmother in the same dreadful year; watched her own face in the mirror grow thinner, sharper, and wondered what was to become of her. The flat in Highgate seemed more home to her than the houses in Chelsea and Somerset, and the time she spent there more real, more important than the time she spent being Charles's wife. Lies and deceit became so much second nature to her (she who had always been so truthful, so direct) that she quite often found herself wondering who precisely she was and where exactly she was supposed to be.

And then one day, Nell realised it was actually rather more than four weeks since she had last had a period. She bought a kit and did a test, and found she was pregnant.

'Well never mind,' said Nick tenderly, holding her while she wept, moaned, rocked with grief. 'It's not so bad. I hate to think about it, but presumably you still sleep with the Prince. It's probably his.'

'No,' said Nell, looking up at him, her face ravaged with tears. 'No, you don't understand. He's had a vasectomy.'

*   *   *

'Now can I just get this straight?' said Charles. He was horribly, hideously calm. 'You've been having an affair. You're pregnant. And the father of your child doesn't want to marry you.'

Nell looked back, equally calm, surprised by her own courage.

'Yes. That's exactly right.'

'I may be a little old-fashioned, but what reason does he give?'

'I don't think I want to talk about that,' said Nell, crushing with sheer force of will the memory of Nick looking dramatically distraught, saying that of course he loved her, he always would, but he couldn't actually marry her, couldn't even take her permanently into his home, because—well, oh it was so hard for him to explain, but . . .

'But what, Nick?' she had said, discovering exactly what people meant when they said that fear clutched at their hearts: her own felt stilled, halted; icy fingers closed round it, squeezing it so it could beat no more.

112

'Well, darling, what kind of a husband would I make? What kind of a father? Feckless, useless, virtually unemployed, broke . . .'

'You don't seem exactly broke,' said Nell carefully, afraid of antagonising him even while rage and pain broke over her in equal proportions. 'You seem to be doing rather nicely actually. You've got that extremely expensive car, lots of new clothes; you've just been on that holiday to Mexico . . .'

'Ella, darling, please!' His dark eyes were hurt, shocked even. 'That's the first holiday I've had for five years. Surely you don't begrudge me that. And I do need the odd shirt, you know. I can't go round dressed in rags, and I don't have a rich husband or even a fairy godmother to buy me things. But darling, it's you I'm thinking of, not me. What kind of life can I offer you and a baby, living here in this garret?'

'It's not a garret,' cried Ella in anguish. 'It's lovely. I'd adore it, and besides, I'd get something from Charles, obviously, and . . .'

She looked at him and saw an expression deep in his eyes, beyond the careful hurt and concern; it was wariness, watchfulness. He was fighting to survive, looking for an escape, and in that moment she knew there was no hope, no hope for her at all, and that while he had been the love of her life, she was nothing of the sort to him, just a foolish, spoilt wife, bored into adultery and probably boring him as well by now.

She took a deep breath and met his eyes, those clever actor's eyes, and said, 'Well, Nick, there's clearly no point in continuing this discussion. You're right, I would hate it. Now that I know how

113

you really feel, I won't trouble you any further. Goodbye. Don't bother to show me out.'

'Ella!' he said, genuinely concerned now. 'Darling Ella, you can't just go. I love you, I need you. Listen, darling, you don't have to have this baby, you know. We are living in the twentieth century. Have you thought about . . . Sweetheart, don't look at me like that. It upsets me . . .'

'Well I'm truly sorry about that,' said Nell, white-hot rage whipping through her, wondering if she might actually hit him. 'I really would hate to think that anything I did might upset you, Nick. I did think about it, having an abortion, of course I did, and I'll tell you what I thought: it was that there's only one person truly innocent in all this hideous mess, and that's the baby. I'm afraid I couldn't do that, Nick, not even to save you from feeling upset.'

'Ella, darling, don't be angry. I didn't mean . . . Oh God, why can't we just . . .'

'We, as you put it, can't do anything,' said Nell. 'There was never any question of any "we" in your life. There's only one person in your life, Nick Buitoni, and always will be, and you're very welcome to him.'

The pleasure she got out of delivering that sentence and the expression of profound shock on his face helped to see her out of the flat and into her car. She had actually reached Chester Square and the safe haven of her own bedroom before the agony of what was undoubtedly the final parting from him actually hit her. And then she had to talk to Charles.

*   *   *

He was icily ruthless with her. He told her he would like her to leave as soon as possible, and that he hoped she wasn't nurturing any idea that she could take Flora and James with her. 'I shall fight you for custody if you try and get them. You can obviously visit them regularly; I won't stand in your way. I shall make you a generous allowance; you won't starve, or be homeless. I don't want to be accused of parsimony. But I would prefer not to see you except on occasions like the children's birthdays, when I hope we can be civilised for their sakes.'

'Oh, don't worry, Charles,' said Nell. 'I've seen some very uncivilised behaviour over the past few years. I think I know how not to behave, at least.'

He looked almost as shocked and discomfited as Nick had.

He was, in absolute terms, very generous. He bought her the lease on a small cottage she had found and fallen in love with in Battersea, made her an annual allowance which provided her with the bread and butter of life (although very little jam), and allowed her to have the children to stay for one weekend a month. Nell didn't contest any of this. She knew that she was in danger of being worse off (Charles having instant access to the finest legal advice in the country), and besides, she didn't have the heart.

1984

Sarah Jane Coleman was born at the West London Hospital with the absolute minimum of discomfort, and lay on her mother's breast looking up at her with eyes as large and velvety-dark as her father's.

115

'They're going to haunt me, those eyes,' said Nell tenderly.

'What was that, Mrs Coleman?' said the midwife. 'Nothing wrong, is there? She's beautiful.'

'No, nothing wrong,' said Nell, stroking the tiny nose, smiling at the waving frond-like fingers, love surging through her, sweetly powerful. 'Nothing wrong at all. Unless you count looking just like her father.'

The midwife, who was very much from the new school, laughed.

Nell rather enjoyed her stay in hospital. She had been bored after the births of Flora and James, lying alone in her flower-filled room at the London Clinic; she found the bustle of the public ward, hearing the life stories, watching the families pour in to meet their new members, enchanting.

Everyone was very nice to her; she was in a majority in the ward in having no husband, although most people had far more visitors. A few loyal friends popped in once or twice, although most of their circle had inevitably sided with Charles. Mary Harris, her next-door neighbour from Battersea, who had befriended her and had called the ambulance for her, came nearly every day, bearing clean nightdresses and gossip (and was sent out each time for smoking in the ward), and so did Nell's new friend, Melanie Jeffries. Melanie was a solicitor and had acted for her over the purchase of her house; she had been driven to despair by Nell's passive attitude, had wanted her to fight Charles for more maintenance, but they had become very close despite Nell's refusal, and spent long giggly evenings in Nell's small front room, plotting the downfall of men in general, and the two in Nell's life and the one in Melanie's in particular.

*   *   *

Sarah Jane was a very good baby. She took her duties seriously, and slept, ate and grew with admirable efficiency. Nell, struggling against loneliness and a financial situation that was challenging, if not exactly hard, added gratitude to the other more conventional maternal emotions. The days were all right; she cared for the baby, shopped and cooked and cleaned her little house. But the evenings were endlessly silent and solitary, apart from the one or two a week she spent with Melanie. Sometimes she could pass twenty-four hours without exchanging a single word with anyone.

She very seldom saw Charles, communicating with him almost entirely through his secretary and the nanny; Nick Buitoni wrote occasional letters, and sent her a huge bouquet of flowers when Sarah Jane was born. Nell sent them back and ignored his letters, but she was shocked to find how much she missed him still. The initial hurt had healed, but the scars were still horribly fresh: fresh enough to send her into paroxysms of grief when she read a story in the *Daily Mail* about him and his new live-in lover, described in the article as 'lovely leggy society beauty Candida Curtis', who had heard his cabaret at the Savoy and fallen head over heels in love with him.

'The nearest she's been to society is when her gran joined the Co-op,' said Melanie tartly. 'Nell, darling, don't, don't cry so much. He's a filthy,

117

faithless jerk, and hopefully Candida will make him very unhappy. Did you know about that song, incidentally?'

'What song?' said Nell, turning a ravaged face back to Melanie.

'It says here he wrote a song a year or two back which he does in cabaret called—let me see—"Cinderella", and it's just won some award or other.'

'Oh yes,' said Nell, very quietly. 'Yes, I know about that song.'

And the memory of listening to Nick playing it on his old piano, reciting the terrible words, smiling at her, hurt so much, was so fierce, she thought she was actually going to faint.

It went on all summer, the song, playing endlessly, haunting her, actually reaching the number twelve slot before finally fading into the obscurity she longed for. 'I think you should do something with your life,' said Melanie, as Sarah Jane slept in her determined way and they munched pizzas and half watched a terrible miniseries on television. 'You're much too bright to sit around being a kept woman. Didn't you ever think of training for something?'

'No,' said Nell humbly. 'I never did. I just met bloody Prince Charming and got married.'

'Well, it's never too late. Look at you, you're lonely and you're bored. It's a terrible waste. Doesn't anything appeal to you?'

Nell thought for a bit. Then: 'Yes,' she said, surprising even herself. 'What you do appeals to me a lot.'

*   *   *

Shortly after Sarah Jane's first birthday, Nell wrote (after much prompting from Melanie) to London University, asking them about the possibility of reading law as a mature student. To her astonishment, they told her she had the necessary A levels. Charles was plainly and interestingly furious when she told him. She enrolled at King's College in October of 1985, nervous, fearful of failure, protesting that she would not be able to cope with the work, that Sarah Jane would suffer; but Melanie drove her on, alternately bullying and encouraging her, and Mary Harris said she would look after Sarah Jane while she was in lectures, promising on her grandmother's grave not to smoke while she did so. Nell had a feeling that the grandmother might have turned in her grave a few times, but on the whole, Mary clearly made an enormous effort.

Charles refused to give Nell any more money, so she sold her rather battered old Renault 5 to pay Mary. Melanie was beside herself with rage, and wanted to take Charles to court, but Nell said she couldn't afford to run the car anyway, it was nothing but a liability, and she'd decided to get a bicycle instead. She cycled up to the Strand whenever the weather was half nice, and as soon as Sarah Jane was old enough, she got a little seat for her on the back for weekends. Sarah Jane loved it, and when James and Flora came to visit, James brought his own bike, greatly to his father's irritation, and they cycled round Battersea Park together, though Flora, who was by now a slightly sanctimonious eight-year-old, said it was very dangerous and waited for them in Mary's house until they got back. There was a phone call from Charles next day to say that if Nell was going to leave the children unsupervised, their visits would have to cease.

Nell loved the course; she had the kind of carefully enquiring and retentive mind that was entirely appropriate to the law, and even the areas she had expected to find dry and possibly dull she discovered to be wonderfully engaging. Her essays, after a rather faltering start, were thoughtful as well as thorough, original as well as sound; her confidence grew, she laughed more, worried less, and realised with surprise as her first year neared its end that she had hardly thought about Nick Buitoni for weeks, and then with a kind of cheerful contempt.

'Told you,' said Melanie when she graduated. 'I'm beginning to wish I'd never encouraged this. I'll have to look out when you finally hit the firms.'

'Don't be silly,' said Nell. 'I only got a two-two.'

'Bloody impressive, with a baby to look after and a mean pig of a husband who doesn't give you enough money for even a week's holiday. Honestly, Nell, I just don't understand why you don't—'

'Melanie, I treated him very badly,' said Nell briefly. 'That's why I don't.'

'He treated you badly.'

'No he didn't. Not by his lights. And I don't want to take any more of his beastly money than I have to. The minute I really qualify, I'm not going to take another farthing from him.'

'You're mad,' said Melanie fondly.

Spring 1994

'Eleanor, are you free? I'd like to talk to you about a new client.'

'Yes, of course,' said Eleanor, smiling carefully at David Bruce with what she hoped was the right mixture of professional cool and personal warmth. David was not only her immediate boss and mentor; he was very sexy in a rather serious way, divorced, plainly lonely, and engaging her sensibilities to an alarming degree. 'Give me ten minutes and I'll be in.'

'Good. It's a very interesting case. I think it would suit you.'

She had become Eleanor when she had been applying for her articles; it seemed more appropriate, more grown-up than Nell. She liked being Eleanor; she felt for the first time in her life that she was a person she could respect. She had worked for Bruce, Lowe Higgins for four years, four happy, absorbing years, and had just been made, to her immense pride, a junior, albeit salaried, partner. She still lived in the little house in Battersea, rather more expensively decorated these days; and she had even bought herself a car, although she still cycled to work occasionally when the morning looked promising enough. Sarah Jane was at a state primary school in Battersea; she was funny, charming and extremely pretty, with what Eleanor perceived as a distressing musical talent. She played the piano and the saxophone with great skill, and sang beautifully; she was also a wonderful mimic—Sarah Jane being Melanie berating the male race, or Mary frantically hiding a lit cigarette, made Eleanor weep with laughter.

James adored her, and loved the time he spent at the little house; but Flora, to her mother's grief, hated Sarah Jane and was slowly becoming estranged from them all.

She scarcely saw Charles; she was forced to see quite a lot about Buitoni in the papers. He had become famous, as much for the string of pretty girls on his arm at first nights as for the three successful musicals he had now written. It enraged Eleanor that these articles still had the power to wound her.

Bruce's, as it was known in the legal fraternity, was a small, young City firm, fast gaining a reputation for its skill in the libel area; Eleanor had worked successfully on several cases now, the most recent being against a women's magazine that had managed to imply in the most simpering adulatory copy that her client, a young actress, was not only an alcoholic, but extremely stupid with it. It had brought her some notoriety, and she had been interviewed with her client on a morning television programme and said absolutely nothing while appearing to say a great deal.

'Well now,' said David Bruce, 'let me tell you about this case. It's basically about plagiarism. Funny chap, name of Richardson, says he wrote a song that's been stolen from him. Years ago, apparently, and he'd given up any hope of getting satisfaction; tried a couple of times, but then met our friend Archie Tremain QC at a party, who told him he really ought to go for it, told him he'd act for him even. I suppose he thought it would be fun; there'll be a lot of publicity, I would think.'

'Goodness,' said Eleanor. 'It sounds intriguing. There must be a lot at stake. What's the song?'

'Never heard of it myself,' said David Bruce, 'but my secretary had. One of these Lloyd-Webber-type numbers. It's called "Cinderella".'

*   *   *

Jack Richardson was a shabbily good-looking man in his early thirties, with only shadows of the handsome boy who had dreamed of being a star. He had, he told Eleanor, been working as a video salesman for the past five years.

'You left showbiz, then?'

'Yes, in despair. I knocked around the business, auditioned endlessly, never got anything; you can't imagine how tough it is.'

'I think I can,' said Eleanor. 'Actually. Now, let's begin at the beginning, shall we?'

Jack Richardson had written the song, he said, for an audition for a cabaret slot on one of the big liners. 'I thought it might help if I did something original.' It hadn't. He couldn't remember the date of the audition, only that it was sometime in the spring of '83, 'at some terrible rehearsal room in South London, now a supermarket. Who'd have a record of that? How could I possibly find anyone else who was there, who might remember?' Richardson's agent at the time was little use as a witness: 'drank himself to death'.

Nick Buitoni had been at the audition too, had heard Richardson sing; they'd chatted briefly. Now he denied ever being there, said he'd been in the States at the time. His agent confirmed it. Eighteen months later, when he had his surprise hit with 'Cinderella', Richardson had written to him and told him the song was his. Buitoni had ignored his

123

letter. 'Of course I didn't have much written down, just meaningless scribbles, and he'd obviously changed bits here and there. Who'd believe that?'

'I would,' said Eleanor.

'This whole thing,' said David Bruce with a sigh, as they discussed it late one night, 'hangs on Richardson not just being able to prove that Buitoni heard the bloody song, but that he was actually at the audition at all. All those years ago. It looks impossible.'

'Nothing's impossible,' said Eleanor.

The case became a cause célèbre; it caught the public fancy. The various witnesses were theatre in themselves. Buitoni was impressive: charming, relaxed, slightly amused. Why should he stoop to such a thing? He was hugely successful in his own right, had already had his first hit, 'Wintersong' (albeit slightly more modest), when 'Cinderella' came out; it was ridiculous. He might have met Richardson, but he certainly didn't remember him—who could possibly recall every crossed path in twenty years in show business? The jury nodded knowingly, as if they spent much of their time in auditions. Buitoni's agent was sincerity itself, an English gentleman to his well-kept fingertips ('Oh for a flash Harry!' groaned Eleanor when she first saw him). Of course Mr Buitoni had written the song himself; he could remember him coming in, slightly apologetically, with an early draft. He had sung the now-famous words to him across the desk, and they had both laughed, then agreed they had a potential hit.

Richardson was nervous, pale; he sounded whingeing. It was the word of one man against the other. Public sympathy was firmly behind the hero, behind Prince Charming, as the tabloids called him.

*   *   *

Eleanor was unprepared for her emotions when she first saw Nick Buitoni in court. She had expected to feel tough and distant and cool; she felt instead frail and involved and shaken. She wondered what she was doing; why she had ever agreed to take him on. Memories of love, long buried, surfaced painfully, agonisingly. Against every instinct, she did not want to be the one who defeated him. And then one day as she walked out of the law courts, down the Strand, he confronted her, half smiling, half rueful, totally confident that she would want to talk to him.

'I can't believe you're doing this,' he said. 'After everything we had.'

'I can,' she said. 'After everything you had.'

Suddenly the case turned. Archie Tremain QC, acting for Jack Richardson, said he would like to call Miss Patrice Prentice.

Patrice Prentice was an ex-Tiller girl. She had been at the audition; she remembered it because she had been successful, got a season on the liner. She also remembered Buitoni well, because she had rushed in late and he had been kind to her, helped her get out her music, held her wrap while she danced.

'And Richardson, do you remember him?'

'Yes, because they told him to wait, then they changed their minds. He was very dejected.'

'Do you remember the song?'

'No, I'm afraid I don't. Not really. I'm sorry.'

'Thank you, Miss Prentice. You've been very helpful indeed.'

It wasn't exactly conclusive, but it was impressive; it made Buitoni appear considerably less reliable as a witness. Archie Tremain made much of it in his final speech; the judge referred to it in his summing-up.

The jury had been out for seven hours when they finally brought in their verdict that Nick Buitoni was guilty of plagiarism; Richardson was awarded a quarter of a million pounds, with costs.

*   *   *

Later, much later, after a great deal of champagne had been drunk at the Savoy, and Jack Richardson had finally departed with his new agent to discuss contracts, David Bruce took Eleanor out to dinner and told her he'd like to buy her many more if she'd let him. She said not unless she was allowed to buy him an equal number: 'I'm an independent creature, David, you have to understand that.'

'Well so long as you'll be independent alongside me, I think I can handle it.'

'Good,' said Eleanor, smiling at him, feeling happiness filling her, warming her.

'Good case,' he said, raising a glass to her. 'Well done. Marvellous, the way you unearthed Miss Prentice like that. I still can't imagine how you knew she was there that day.'

'Oh,' said Eleanor thoughtfully, thinking of the yellowing scrap of paper she had never quite been able to throw away: the running order for an audition, with the first terrible words of 'Cinderella' scribbled on the back. 'Just think of it as a variation on the glass slipper story. And this one fitted rather well.'

THE BEACH HUT

It had been the most wonderful love affair. Wild and amazing, begun while they were both still students. Michael and Clara: Michael a writer and a dreamer, much given to penning sweet, silly poems dedicated to Clara, a fashion designer with dreams of becoming the next Vivienne Westwood. He would whisk her off on sudden romantic idylls; most notably to a windswept beach on the north Cornish coast called Trebewick, where they stayed in a rickety wooden building little better than a beach hut and consummated their relationship for the first time, while the sea roared outside.

As in all the best love affairs, they promised to stay together for ever, and indeed they had, or for twenty years certainly; and they still loved each other very much, despite certain changes in circumstance, like Michael becoming a smooth-talking and very successful ad man, earning big bucks, with a fondness for five-star hotels set preferably on the Mediterranean coast, while Clara was the chief buyer for a large, middle-market clothes chain; moreover they had a beautiful house filled with stylish things and really lacked for very little.

They had raised three very nice sons, one of whom was at university and two at school, the youngest (by seven years) an afterthought—'the last time conception was even likely', Clara was given to saying, rather untruthfully, but wanting to make a point of their flagging sex life. The sex life that had been so wild and wonderful, conducted on beaches and clifftops, in woodland clearings and on river banks, simply because they couldn't wait a second longer, even if it was raining or blowing a gale. And sometimes Clara would lie in bed, as Michael slept deeply and noisily beside her, and thought of the little wooden cottage in Trebewick and the guttering oil lamp and the way their skin tasted of salt and their hair had tangled together in the wild wind, and wondered quite how things could have changed so absolutely.

Their twentieth wedding anniversary was approaching; Michael didn't seem even to have remembered it. Clara was not so much hurt as disappointed, and filled with a rather destructive restlessness.

And so it came to pass that Seth came into her life. Seth was a young designer whose work she had encouraged and even featured in a couple of major promotions. He reminded her of the young Michael, with his wild curly hair and intense nature; she rather feared she must remind him of his mother. But one evening, over a glass of champagne to celebrate his first big order, he told her that he found her extremely attractive—'You're a lot sexier than you let on,' he added, smiling at her with a strange assurance. 'I mean, why the midi skirt when you have legs like men dream about? And the schoolmarmy up-do? You should let it all hang out—would you take out those clips for me, let me see . . .'

And half mesmerised, Clara pulled out the combs that held her hair high on the back of her head and shook out a gleaming dark brown mane.

'Cool,' was all he said, nodding with satisfaction, taking another sip of his champagne. Shortly afterwards, he went back to the basement flat he inhabited in his parents' house, not yet being successful enough to set so much as a toe on the property ladder, and she drove home to the large, immaculate house in Fulham feeling as if a wild west wind was stirring somewhere at the back of her heart.

Time passed; the anniversary drew closer, three months, then two; she dropped hints about it to Michael: 'Oh yes,' he said, 'our twentieth, getting nearer, isn't it? Got any ideas?'

It was not, she thought, clenching her teeth, for her to have the ideas.

And so one afternoon, with the anniversary six weeks away, and the same hints met with the same dull, bland response, when Seth invited her to lunch with him the next day to celebrate a big editorial in a glossy magazine, she accepted with almost no hesitation at all; and found herself the next morning picking out an above-the-knee skirt teamed with a silk T-shirt which had a tendency to emphasise her nipples, and a waterfall cardigan in softest cashmere. She left her hair falling to her shoulders and not a comb in sight.

Lunch was very sexy; a dangerous meal at the best of times, with its cover of midday innocence. She found herself almost unable to swallow as Seth's knee nudged repeatedly against hers under the table, and completely unable to stop smiling foolishly as his dark eyes probed hers and he told her she looked 'yeah, unbelievably sexy'.

Lunch was followed by another lunch another day, and ever more frequent drinks after work; she began arriving home late at least two nights a week. Nobody cared; Michael very often worked

129

late too, the housekeeper always prepared the boys' evening meal, and when she did get home, she found them as she always did, earphones clamped to their heads, eyes glued to their computer screens, assuring her they were working on their projects, which as she tartly remarked were unlikely to be entitled 'War Zone' or 'Aliens Reach Earth'. However, where once she would have ordered the earphones off and the screens blanked, now she smiled vaguely at them and wandered into the kitchen to pour herself another glass of wine, hoping rather than fearing to find Michael out.

With three weeks to go to the anniversary and Michael telling her to 'remind me to book a table somewhere that night', a suggestion that after their drinks she should drop Seth home—'I'm fine, truly, I only had one glass of wine'—became a prolonged parking up in a side street. She wondered rather wildly what would happen if they were seen and even challenged (headlines in the paper: 'Top fashion buyer in compromising situation with toy-boy designer'), before abandoning herself to the almost forgotten pleasure of snogging in the car, and the stirrings of the heartfelt west wind becoming a hurricane.

And thus to the inevitable: 'Could you maybe get away one night?' and 'Maybe, you'll have to let me think about it', the temptation beyond endurance, the sweet anxiety of the plotting and alibi planting, discovering a conference far enough away to demand an overnight stay, the glorious piercing of guilt. One night, a few days before the conference and the anniversary only ten days away, she mentioned it to Michael as a kind of test.

'Oh God,' was all he said. 'I still haven't booked

anywhere. Why don't you do it? You always like to choose the restaurant anyway.'

That did it; he deserved it. God only knew where this relationship with Seth was taking her, but she just didn't care. She wanted to be valued and desired and above all cared about again, the security of marriage suddenly and shockingly less important.

As she was packing her bag—new nightdress, long and floaty to disguise the undoubted southward drift of her boobs and stomach, richly fragranced oil for the shared bath Seth had rather graphically pictured for her, some scented candles in case they were not provided by the hotel, which she had booked close enough to the conference to make sense, far enough away to make any sightings by colleagues unlikely—she felt a stab of sheer panic. How would she cope with the sex, the demands of a young man who was used, no doubt, to the gorgeous firm bodies and skilful performances of girls literally half her age? What was she doing, who did she think she was?

Then she looked at the two pictures of Michael she kept by her bed, one of the wild-haired, burning-eyed young poet, the other a portrait of the handsome, middle-aged cliché he had become, so careless of the marking of twenty years of marriage that he couldn't be bothered even to book a restaurant table to celebrate it, and she knew exactly what she was doing and who she was—a still sexy, still hungry forty-something who was grasping at adventure before it was too late.

She picked the bag up and went down to the hall, left the note she had written for the housekeeper detailing exactly what the boys should have for their supper—chicken lasagne, their favourite, and Ben & Jerry's strawberry cheesecake; she didn't want them feeling neglected or miserable. She was just going to scribble a cool note for Michael saying goodbye and she'd see him the following evening when the landline rang.

She frowned: hardly worth bothering; no one she cared about would use it, except her mother, and she was the last person on earth Clara wanted to speak to this morning. Then she thought of the one other person who it might be: Janet, the housekeeper, calling in sick—please, please God, no—and went back in and rather tentatively picked it up.

'Mr Wentworth there?' It was a voice with a burr of an accent; what was it? Devon? Somerset? No, bit more of an edge.

'No,' she said briskly. 'He's at work. I'll give you his mobile.'

'We tried that. No answer.'

'Oh. Well he must be in a meeting. You could try later.'

'Can't wait till later. We got a day's work ahead, can't afford to waste the time.'

'Well—I don't know what to suggest.'

'Maybe you could help. It's about where to deliver this wood and stuff.'

'The wood? There must be some mistake. We don't have any open fires.'

'It's not to burn, missus.' The voice sounded amused. 'It's to build with.'

'Build what? I don't understand.'

'The hut. The hut by the beach.'

'The beach? What beach?'

'Trebewick. Where he wants this hut built. Only

132

we can't get to it. We can see where he means, but there's no clearing, not really, all overgrown it is, and what looks like half another hut, all crumbling away. Be two days' work before we can start putting this one up. So is he going to pay for that or what? We need to speak to him. Otherwise we'll have to dump this lot and go.'

'Did you say Trebewick?' said Clara. She felt very odd suddenly.

'That's it, yes. Funny old place this is, fair way from the village; why he wants a beach hut put up here Lord alone knows, but anyway, that's not for us to argue about. All I know is it's got to be up and doing in a week's time, and that means he's got to OK the extra money right now.'

'Well . . .' Clara's mind had cleared. 'Well, I think I can say he—he certainly would OK it. In fact, I'll give you the authority myself. Charge me now if you want; I'll give you my card details.'

'That'd be welcome.'

'But could you do me a favour: don't call him. Just get the hut up, and if he calls you, don't mention that we talked. I—I remember it all now and he'll—he'll be annoyed that I've forgotten.'

'OK.' The voice was amused. 'Don't want to cause trouble between man and wife, that's for sure.'

'No, no, that wouldn't be a good idea at all,' said Clara, smiling, reaching for her wallet.

*   *   *

Ten minutes later she was on her way to work, still smiling. Not before she had texted Seth, to say sorry, but she couldn't meet him after all, not tonight, not at all, and she'd try to explain later. He'd be a little upset, but not for long. There would be plenty of firm-bodied, sexually skilful girls to console him. And he wouldn't understand her explanation one bit.

THE BROOCH

It was a very beautiful brooch. It was what used to be called paste, and now would be called diamanté: glittery and brilliant and in the shape of a full moon with two stars trailing off it on two slender threads. It was the sort of thing you could make stories up about, which Anna had when she was little— like the moon wearing the stars as a sort of sash. Or the stars were trying to get away from it. The brooch belonged to her grandmother, Bella, and was pinned to her large, cushiony bosom, and Anna would sit on her knee and play with it. Later on, she had been allowed to wear it when they went to tea with her and she would keep saying she wanted to go to the lavatory so she could pass the big mirror in the hall and admire it, pinned on to her cardigan, right in the middle of her small, flat chest. One day, she thought, she would have wonderful bosoms like her grandmother and the brooch would show up much better. She had always known she would have the brooch; her grandmother had promised her that, adding quickly that Rachel, Anna's older sister, would have her pearls.

*   *   *

Rachel wasn't really in the least interested in either the brooch or the pearls; she was a tomboy and only cared about getting into the school teams and climbing trees like the boys, but she did mind that Anna was so clearly the favourite and so she used to make a great fuss and demand to be allowed to wear the brooch too. She didn't really want to, but making Anna miserable made her feel a bit better. Rachel wasn't pretty like Anna, who had fair curls and big blue eyes; she had dark, straight hair, brown eyes and almost sallow skin, but she did much better at school; she was sharp and clever, and she wanted to be a doctor when she grew up.

*   *   *

The girls had never got on; their mother, Diana, often said they were fighting in their playpen. Rachel had a sharp tongue and a quick temper, but her method of attack—usually a kick or a bite—was swift and swiftly over; Anna could bear a grudge for hours or even days, and she could hold her tears back until her mother was in earshot, and then suddenly wail and clutch her injury to get the maximum mileage from it. Rachel was almost always in trouble.

*   *   *

The only person who always stuck up for her was her Grandpa George. 'She's got such spirit,' he would say fondly. He was a bit suspicious of Anna and her wide blue eyes; 'We know all about her,' he would say winking at Rachel, 'bit too good to be true, isn't she?' Rachel adored him back; it made up for the fuss Grandmother Bella made of Anna.

In 1960, when Anna was seven and Rachel eight, Grandmother Bella died. It was a terrible shock; she was only fifty-eight. 'She's too young to die', people kept saying at the funeral. The girls thought this ridiculous; fifty-eight was terribly old. But the most shocked person—of course—was Grandpa George, who was ten years older than Bella and had not expected to have to endure a lonely old age. For a long time he was broken-hearted, pining for his Bella in their big empty house. The only person able to comfort him was Rachel, and she would go over most Sundays to see him, taking him for walks, making him take her for drives, playing Scrabble with him (his favourite game) and usually winning, keeping him up to date with the new pop music. Everyone said how wonderful she was, which made Anna very cross. Not only had she lost her grandmother, she had lost her role as star grandchild. She spent a lot of time sobbing loudly in her room whenever Rachel set off to visit Grandpa George.

*   *   *

One of the things that had happened, because of Grandmother Bella dying so young, was that she hadn't ever made a will. Not that it terribly mattered—she and Daddy shared everything, Diana said sadly—but there was one thing that came to matter very much. Grandpa George called Rachel into his study one day. 'Something for you,' he said. 'Something I want you to have. It was Granny Bella's favourite and I know she'd want you to have it if she knew what a comfort you've been.

136

Here, darling. With my love.' And there it was, in a little box: the moon and stars brooch.

It was very difficult. Even Diana was upset. 'Anna was told she could have that brooch,' she said to Rachel. 'She's going to be broken-hearted.' Which made Rachel cross.

'It's me that's cheered Grandpa up,' she said.

'I know, darling, but—'

'And he wants me to have it. It would be horrible to tell him he's got it wrong.'

Richard, their father, agreed. 'For God's sake, Diana, Anna's only seven. She can have some other trinket. I'll have a word with George.' Which he did, and Anna was duly given the seed pearl necklace.

*   *   *

She was furious: so furious that for days she could hardly eat. It was so unfair. That brooch was hers: Granny Bella had promised her. Rachel didn't want it—she'd rather have a new hockey stick.

'I do want it,' said Rachel. 'I jolly well do. And Grandpa George wants me to have it. So just shut up about it. It's mine.'

*   *   *

She never wore it, of course. But she would never lend it to Anna. As the girls grew up, into flower power fashion and thence the floaty romanticism of the seventies, Anna longed to have it, to pin it to one of her Biba hats, or her Laura Ashley bodices, but Rachel just said no. It was hers; Grandpa George wanted her to have it. The only times she

137

did wear it were for Grandpa George's visits and on the dreadful day of his funeral, when it seemed to help. Otherwise it stayed in her drawer, in its box. She took it with her when she went to Cambridge to study medicine.

Anna didn't go to university; she went to teacher-training college. She said being a teacher would fit in better with having her own children. Rachel was very scornful and said it was a pathetic reason to choose a career. Rachel was very successful with men. They came flocking to her door from the time she was about fifteen. Pretty, sweet-faced Anna did less well; in fact, by the age of twenty she still hadn't had a proper boyfriend.

'Rachel has sex appeal, as your mother used to call it,' said Richard, smiling when Diana fretted over this. 'It's just something in her. Don't fuss. Anna will find Mr Right. Give her time.'

*   *   *

Rachel was in love—with someone from Cambridge, a very good-looking and charming someone, who seemed to like her, but had never asked her out. She was incensed; it had never happened to her before. 'It's exactly because you're not sure of him that you like him so much,' her mother said.

'It isn't!' cried Rachel in agony. 'He's the best-looking bloke in my year, in any year. And he's so funny and sexy. I know how Anna feels, now, never getting a man.'

'Rachel, be quiet!' said Diana sharply. But it was too late: Anna had heard her. She fled to her room in tears.

138

*　　　*　　　*

Two days later, a miracle happened. Two miracles, actually. The good-looking and charming someone, whose name was Lucas, asked Rachel to go to a big dinner party with him. And the same night, Anna was invited to the college Christmas Ball by the one boy in her year she fancied. 'It's just too good to be true,' Diana said happily. Richard, who had taken to calling her Mrs Bennett, was very amused.

*　　　*　　　*

'You know what would look wonderful with that?' said Diana as Rachel showed her the low-cut black velvet dress she planned to wear. 'Granny's brooch.'

Rachel rummaged in her drawer, found the box and pinned it on the dress, at its lowest point, where it nestled, lighting up her cleavage.

'You're right,' she said.

Diana thought thankfully of the floaty chiffon creation that Anna was wearing; there was no way she'd want to wear anything sparkly on it. Only Anna did—not on the dress, but she had read an article in *Vogue* which said that the place for sparkle was in your hair. *Ransack Granny's jewellery box*, it said, and showed something very similar to the moon and stars brooch.

Anna bought a couple of slides from Fenwicks, and they did look quite nice, but . . . She took a deep breath and asked Rachel, really very nicely, if she could possibly borrow the brooch. Rachel said no.

'You're so mean,' said Anna. 'It's not as if you're

going to wear it.'

'I am, actually,' said Rachel, 'aren't I, Mummy?'

Diana nodded, rather unhappily.

Rachel gave Anna a distinctly crushing smile. 'So sorry,' she said.

They quarrelled noisily for at least another half-hour before Anna gave up.

*   *   *

Anna left for the evening long before Rachel did; she looked lovely, they all agreed. Even Rachel said so. 'And those slides are perfect.'

'Well, they're all right,' said Anna.

'Isn't lover boy going to collect you?'

Anna flushed. 'No. He lives miles away. He's meeting me there.'

'I'll take you, darling,' said Richard.

'No, honestly, it's fine; lots of us are going to share a cab. I'm first pick-up . . .'

'Well, have a lovely time,' said Diana.

'I will. Thank you.' And she was gone.

*   *   *

A howl of rage came from Rachel's bedroom half an hour later. The brooch wasn't in her drawer. It wasn't anywhere. They searched every corner of every room—including Anna's. Well, Rachel did.

'She's got it,' she said, tears of rage filling her eyes. 'Cow. She knew how much tonight matters. I hate her. I thought she looked funny, when she left. She couldn't wait to get out of the house. Bitch.'

'Rachel, darling—'

'Don't "darling" me. She must have it, she must.

Oh God, there's the bell; is my mascara running? Oh, I hate her so much.'

*   *   *

Rachel came down to Sunday breakfast pale and heavy-eyed. The evening had not been a success.

'It's your fault,' she said to a rather subdued Anna. 'I was so upset about the brooch, I couldn't think of anything else. I don't know how you could have done it, Anna; you really are a prize cow.'

'Rachel, I did not take the brooch.'

'Of course you did. Don't lie about it. And where is it now? Where have you hidden it?'

'I hate you,' said Anna suddenly, her voice heavy with emotion. 'I absolutely hate you.'

'And I hate you. You're pathetic; you're a liar as well as a thief. Anyway, how was your evening? Had your first kiss at last, have you? You must be the oldest virgin in the home counties.'

'Rachel!' said her father. 'Apologise to your sister at once. And don't talk in that disgusting way.'

'I won't apologise. Why should I? She took that brooch and ruined my evening.'

'That is so pathetic,' said Anna. 'It's just a wonderful excuse. You can't bring yourself to admit that someone just didn't fancy you for once. You're not just a tart—you're totally arrogant.'

'I am not a tart!'

'You're a tart. And until you apologise for what you said to me, I'm not going to speak to you.'

'Fine. That's fine by me. It'll be a relief. You never say anything remotely interesting, anyway. No wonder men don't like you. You're just so boring. And desperate. It shows, you know, the way you

141

flirt with everyone—even the milkman—everyone finds it really amusing—'

'Shut up!' shrieked Anna, and fled from the room.

* * *

Diana was sure it would blow over: they were both upset; they often quarrelled. But this time was different and it didn't blow over, and they didn't forgive one another. The wounds were too deep; what had been said was too desperately personal and cruel.

The brooch was never found.

* * *

Six months later, Lucas suddenly invited Rachel out to dinner in Cambridge; he said he'd suddenly realised what a treasure lay within his reach and, after a very token resistance, she forgave him. Within three months they were engaged and a year later, married. It was quite a big wedding; Rachel had no grown-up bridesmaids, just four small ones and four pageboys. It was a convenient reason for her not to have Anna, who wasn't deceived. Diana begged Rachel to rethink: 'It's a very public slap in the face, darling, and she's so upset.'

But Rachel wouldn't. 'After the things she said to me, I don't want her as my bridesmaid. Alright?'

* * *

A year later, Anna was due to get married; David, her husband-to-be, was an extremely nice, if a little dull, teacher at her infants' school. Anna had several grown-up bridesmaids, but Rachel was out of the question, since she was married herself.

'And I don't like the idea of a matron of honour. Sorry, Rachel.'

In neither set of wedding photographs could a shot be found of the sisters together.

*   *   *

The two husbands didn't like each other much and had nothing in common; there was no need for them to meet except at family gatherings. The distance between the sisters grew. Rachel had two boys; Anna, three girls. Neither invited the other to be godmother. Rachel continued to work; Anna stayed at home and, if they did meet, there were always references to the deprived children of working mothers, and the dullness of stay-at-home ones.

*   *   *

Diana struggled down the years to bring the girls together; she suggested joint holidays, gave lots of big birthday parties, and of course there was always Christmas. But, if Rachel was going to be with her parents, Anna seemed to have to spend it with David's. And the other way round.

*   *   *

Then there were holidays: Diana and Richard invited everyone to Tuscany; both families accepted, but at the last minute Lucas phoned and

143

said Rachel wasn't well and couldn't come. Diana told him just to send the children, but he said it would be too much. 'We'll hopefully come out later. When Rachel's better.'

They never arrived.

*   *   *

When they got home, Anna phoned Rachel.

'I do hope you're better,' she said icily. 'I suppose you realise you broke Mummy's heart?'

'You're always so bloody dramatic, Anna. She was fine about it, Lucas said.'

'Oh, really? You don't have a heart yourself, that's your problem. You're a bitch, Rachel. Well, we had a much nicer time without you, I can tell you that.'

'Yes, it must have been so interesting, sitting at the dinner table, listening to David's views on education every night. I do wish we'd been there.'

Anna slammed the phone down.

*   *   *

Next summer, Diana invited just the children to stay with her and Richard in a cottage they rented in Cornwall.

'They're all over five, and we can manage between us; I'd so like them to get to know one another.'

That holiday wasn't a success, either; the children fought relentlessly and, one dreadful day, one of Rachel's boys pushed one of Anna's girls into a rock pool and her leg was so badly cut she had to have stitches.

144

'Like mother, like son,' said Anna icily, when they both arrived to collect the children two days early. Rachel was so genuinely shocked, her eyes filled with tears.

'I was about to apologise for him,' she said. 'He's very sorry too. But just forget it.'

'I wish I could,' said Anna.

*   *   *

It was Diana's sixty-fifth birthday and she was having a party. 'Three-line whip,' Richard said heavily as he phoned with the invitation. 'You're all to behave yourselves.'

He had aged a lot over the years; he looked nearer seventy himself.

Rachel's sons were darkly handsome: the elder, seventeen-year-old Tom, was extremely sexy. Anna's sixteen-year-old, Lizzy, was sweetly pretty. The two of them were found in one of the bedrooms towards the end of the party, both of them half undressed, Tom kissing Lizzy's breasts. No real harm was done, but the ensuing row was frightful, with both sets of parents hurling abuse at one another. Phrases like, 'exactly what I would have expected,' and, 'not as innocent as she looks,' filled the air. Diana, her evening ruined, went to bed in tears.

*   *   *

Richard died in 2000, just a week short of their golden wedding anniversary. His last words to his daughters were, 'Please, you two. Make it up.'

Diana sat, weeping silently, at the funeral, with

145

one girl at either side of her; after everyone had gone, she called the two of them into the drawing room.

'I don't think I could feel more unhappy,' she said, 'but I could face the future a little more easily if you two would be friends. This hostility was one of the things that wore Daddy out. I think it's time you grew up. Please try.'

*   *   *

'I'd like to,' said Rachel to Anna, when they were alone, 'but it's up to you, really. You took the brooch. That's where it all began.'

'It began with you not believing me.'

The reconciliation never got off the ground.

*   *   *

Six months later, Diana put the house on the market; it sold very quickly, and she bought a pretty little Georgian cottage nearer the town. A month later, the new owner rang her; he had had the floorboards taken up in one of the bedrooms and found something he thought might be valuable.

'It's a brooch. Lovely thing, sort of moon and stars.'

*   *   *

Diana called Rachel and told her. 'Do you remember,' she said, 'there was that wide gap between two of the boards near your bed? It created an awful draught. I was so glad to get it carpeted over. The brooch must have slipped down

146

there, off your bed.'

'I remember,' said Rachel. Her voice was rather small. 'I'd better talk to Anna.'

*   *   *

Anna was very gracious. 'I was hardly blameless. I said some awful things to you as well.'

'Yes, you did.'

'Not that you were exactly polite.'

'Well, what did you expect?'

'Rachel,' said Anna wearily, 'it's time I told you the truth.'

'What truth?'

'I didn't need to take the brooch. I didn't go out that night.'

'Of course you went out. I saw you go. All dressed up.'

'Rachel, I went to the cinema. On my own. That boy phoned me and cancelled. Obviously he'd found something better to do. Or someone better to take. I couldn't face telling you. Or anyone. A date at last and it was cancelled. So I got the taxi to the station, got on a train to London, where no one was likely to know me, and went to the latest Bond film. To this day I can't hear that music without feeling sick. Then I just went home again, said I'd had a lovely time and went to bed. And cried most of the night.'

Rachel stared at her; she was rather white.

'Oh my God,' she said. 'How awful. You should have told me—long ago. What can I say, Anna? What can I do?'

'Nothing,' said Anna, smiling sweetly. 'Really, nothing. It's fine.'

'It's not fine. I feel dreadful. Well, look, whatever else, you must have the brooch now. Of course you must. I insist. Really.'

*   *   *

Anna drove home, the brooch in its box on the passenger seat beside her. Every so often she smiled down at it. Pity she had had to wait so long. But she had got it back at last. It had proved a very good hiding place for it. Very good indeed. And it had made her feel just a little better that awful night, knowing Rachel couldn't wear it either . . .

BABY KNOWS BEST

Harriet and Priscilla had been friends since their schooldays, a long and happy association, and although their life paths had been very different, and their husbands particularly so, they had remained close, and indeed lived a few streets away from one another in a leafy Surrey suburb. After school, they had grown apart to a degree, Harriet having become a high-powered solicitor in a City firm, and Priscilla developing her own business making cushions and soft toys, but although their lifestyles were not very compatible, and Harriet's rather formal and smart dinner parties bore little resemblance to Priscilla's big drop-in kitchen suppers, they still met at local and school events, and at least every three months or so convened in one or the other's kitchen to gossip and catch up, as Harriet called it.

They each had one daughter: Priscilla's Poppy, however, having three brothers, enjoyed a rather chaotic childhood and went to the local comprehensive; Harriet's Gemma was a formally raised—and perfectly behaved—only child, entrusted to the care of a nanny while her mother went to work and sent to boarding school when she was eleven.

The girls both married within the same year, but their choice of spouse was very different from what might have been imagined. Poppy—to her parents' considerable chagrin—had fallen in love with Toby, a corporate lawyer, whom she had met at university (where she had switched from sociology to economics), and set up house with him in a smart terrace in north London; while Gemma—to her parents' near-anguish—had settled down with Luke, an unemployed poet, in a commune in Somerset.

It was not too surprising, therefore, that each mother eyed the other's son-in-law with envious eyes.

In due course, and again coincidentally, both girls became pregnant within a few weeks of each other; and after the initial joy of prospective grandmotherhood, Harriet and Priscilla found themselves anxiously considering the different methods of birthing their daughters had chosen. Poppy had opted for an elective Caesarean in a private hospital: 'Mummy, don't look like that. My gynaecologist said there was no way she would put herself through a vaginal delivery. You absolutely don't understand how dangerous it is. And yes, Toby's all for it, says he doesn't want to risk that; besides, it's better for the baby, so much less

149

traumatic, and I can get back to work sooner as well. Please stop fussing.'

Gemma had arranged to give birth under self-hypnosis in a birthing centre, accompanied by a freelance and freethinking midwife and a doula: 'Mummy, don't look like that. You don't understand: all hospitals do is interfere with what is a completely natural process and make it more dangerous and much slower. As for the pain, well, there just isn't any if you handle it properly; you just breathe the baby out. It's how you bond in the very earliest moments. So please stop fussing.'

In the event, Poppy's baby, Benjy, arrived in the world swiftly and easily and two weeks early, in the conventional manner, taking her parents and her obstetrician completely by surprise—'There just wasn't time to get me ready for the section, and actually, I feel fine, but of course I was very lucky'—while Gemma's Tilly had to be whipped out by an emergency Caesarean after thirty-six hours of struggling to breathe her out—'I was just very unlucky, the doula said; she'd never known her method fail before, but at least the baby is fine, and yes, I do feel I've bonded with her, the minute she was put in my arms, though again the doula said that was unusual. Next time I'm sure it'll be fine.'

The two girls settled into early motherhood, with its attendant exhaustion and frustrations. Benjy was to be raised according to the doctrine of Gina Ford, put into his own room from two weeks old and subjected to the discipline of controlled crying, so that he might more quickly be in a routine. 'They prefer it that way,' Poppy said patiently to her mother. 'They're happier and more relaxed, they know where they are, they learn very quickly, and

150

it's much better for their parents. Toby certainly doesn't want a baby snuffling and fussing next to our bed; he needs his sleep.'

Tilly on the other hand was swaddled close to her mother's body wherever she went, had never been lain down in a cot or pram, and slept in her parents' bed, often suckling for what seemed to Luke at least most of the night.

Both babies cried a great deal, whether by the controlled method or not, their exhausted mothers ignoring the advice proffered by their respective grandmothers: that Tilly should be put in the crib that Harriet had bought for her, and left to settle down in peace and tranquillity in her own room for at least a few hours a day; and that Benjy should be held and cuddled more, and his cot moved back into his parents' bedroom, where he would feel safe and reassured.

*   *   *

It was an early spring Saturday when Gemma arrived at her mother's house, Tilly strapped to her breast with a large Indian shawl. The baby appeared uncomfortable, slightly crushed; too big for it really, Harriet thought, and she told Gemma that she had bought her one of the new-generation slings, which would give the baby some support and allow her to face outwards and look at the world. Gemma said she thought they were rather cold and rigid and she didn't really approve of them; Harriet said humbly that it would be there if Gemma wanted it, and asked where Luke was.

'Oh, he's so selfish,' said Gemma irritably. 'He's staying at the commune; he's writing an epic poem he's been invited to read at one of the literary festivals, and he says he can't concentrate with Tilly crying all the time. I don't know how he thinks I can concentrate; I have to listen to it far more than he does . . . Honestly, she never stops crying, even when I've just fed her . . .'

A few roads away, Poppy had arrived at Priscilla's house. She looked exhausted and cross. 'Where's Toby, dear?'

'Don't even speak to me about Toby. He's in the office; he's got what he thinks is some terribly important work to do, says he can't do it at home because of Benjy crying. It's not as if he has to listen to it all day as well.'

Priscilla asked politely how the controlled crying was going. 'Well of course we are getting there, but it's taking a while. Benjy just has to learn who's boss. Sometimes he cries for over an hour before he drops off. It's awful, but one mustn't give in.'

*   *   *

It was a noisy night in both houses; in the morning, Priscilla and Harriet offered to take the babies out so that their daughters could sleep, and rang each other to arrange a meeting in the park.

As she approached the agreed meeting place, trying rather irritably and unsuccessfully to loosen the shawl so that Tilly could see a bit more, Harriet saw Priscilla coming towards her, pushing the pram rather gingerly, as if it contained a hand grenade. Which indeed Priscilla felt it did. Both babies were crying loudly.

Harriet looked at the pram lustfully. 'I just think,' she said, 'that if Tilly could lie quietly for a

152

while, she'd go to sleep and then I could take her home and put her in the garden. She's exhausted, just as much as Gemma; she never gets any rest.'

'Take it, take it,' said Priscilla, whisking Benjy out, 'and lend me that shawl, would you. I'll give him a proper cuddle and walk him round for a bit. He's starved of human contact, literally. Fifteen minutes after each feed and that's it, poor little mite.'

They walked together for a while, smiling serenely, if a little smugly, over the now soundly sleeping babies. Benjy was relaxed, cuddled into his grandmother's capacious bosom, and Tilly was splayed out in the pram, her small arms raised above her head.

'Oh dear,' said Harriet suddenly. 'There's Poppy.'

'And Gemma,' said Priscilla. 'Now we're for it.'

They were. How could they, the two girls demanded, how could their mothers do something so absolutely counter to what they had been told was right for the babies?

'Well yes, dear, but . . .' said Harriet, indicating the sweetly sleeping Tilly.

'I know, darling, but . . .' said Priscilla, stroking the sleeping Benjy's head tenderly.

It was agreed they should all go home immediately.

When Harriet and Gemma got to Harriet's house, it did seem rather dreadful to wake Tilly. Gemma agreed, albeit grudgingly, that she might as well stay in the pram until she woke up. Priscilla suggested, on arriving at her house, that she should cuddle Benjy—also still sleeping soundly—a little longer before putting him in his cot. An hour later,

153

when Poppy had finished checking her emails, he was still fast asleep in his grandmother's arms.

*   *   *

Three weeks later, it was Mother's Day.

Harriet opened her door to see Luke with an enormous bunch of dried grasses in his arms; he handed her an envelope.

'You are a complete star,' he said. 'Happy Mother's Day. Thanks to you, I got my poem finished. Gemma's just coming; got held up chatting to someone.'

Harriet opened the envelope rather nervously, and pulled out a thick piece of white paper, covered in perfect copperplate handwriting. 'Ode to Harriet', it said at the top.

Gemma, looking slightly shamefaced, wheeled a large baby buggy in at the gate. In it lay Tilly, sleeping peacefully.

Priscilla opened her door to see Toby holding a huge and clearly expensive bouquet of white roses. 'These are for you,' he said. 'Happy Mother's Day. I cannot thank you enough. Life suddenly seems bearable again. Poppy, where are you?'

Poppy came into the porch, a baby sling strapped to her front; in it, Benjy was curled up, sleeping peacefully.

*   *   *

That evening, having both resisted saying anything as crude as 'I told you so', Harriet and Priscilla met for a glass of wine.

'Well,' said Harriet, 'we won. Mother really does

154

know best.'

'Of course,' said Priscilla. 'Well, it is Mother's Day.'

But had the babies been able to communicate, they would have agreed that of course *they* were the winners, and that whatever anyone tried to impose on them, it was baby, not mother or father, or childcare expert, or even granny, who actually did know best.

FAIR EXCHANGE

When Jonathan asked Miranda to marry him, he stressed that he was never in the least likely to make a lot of money. People in his line of business—which was carpentry—seldom made a lot of money. And, if Miranda was looking for a big house and a flashy car, she would be well advised to marry someone else, like, for instance, their mutual friend, Murray Kingston, who owned a gallery and famously proposed to her at his annual Christmas Eve party and continued to do so, undeterred by such minor considerations as a wife and now a baby.

The Kingstons lived in a very big house in St John's Wood and had a very flashy car; and not only did Mrs Kingston, whose name was Francesca, have designer clothes, but the baby did, too. They had asked Jonathan to quote for the carpentry in their glitzy new kitchen when they moved into the house, but his estimate came in so far above all the other ones that Murray Kingston, who had not, after all, become rich by throwing all his money away, was forced, very regretfully, to turn it down, not finding the beauty of the work quite sufficient to justify its huge cost; the hope, therefore, that this year Jonathan might earn a little more than his overheads and the most basic financial demands of his family, was once again dashed.

For a long time, Miranda had accepted this; she loved and admired Jonathan so much that not having money and only a very modest home seemed a small price to pay for his adhering to his principles. 'It's much more important that our children have real values,' she was often heard to say, her large brown eyes shining earnestly beneath her shaggy dark fringe, 'than live in a house full of expensive, tacky rubbish.' And Jonathan would kiss her and tell her how much he loved her and how lucky he was to have her.

And if occasionally she longed to have her hair properly styled, like Francesca's, instead of doing it herself, or to buy a slinky new dress for a party instead of climbing into one of her floaty, ethnic cottons, or to drench herself in some expensive scent rather than 'oil of honeysuckle' from the health food store, she would tell herself that, if she did, Jonathan wouldn't like it anyway. He disapproved of sleek, glossy women as much as she despised smart, carefully dressed men. They were, they agreed, perfectly suited and perfectly happy ... And then everything started to go wrong.

Miranda got tired. Very tired. Tired of living in the tiny terraced house with its unfinished kitchen (unfinished because Jonathan only worked on it when he had nothing else to do, which was very rare as he spent most of his time on his wooden sculptures for an exhibition he was planning to give one day). Tired of never being able to go out, not even to the cinema, or on holiday except to self-catering cottages. Tired of having to lug the children round on buses because the old can, which was their only car, was always being used by Jonathan. Tired of pandering to Jonathan's vanity, of pretending she didn't mind any of it, that he and his talent were worth it. Too tired to sparkle for him over the lentil stew when he was downhearted, too tired to make up the big vases of wild flowers and grasses that made the cottage look less drab, and too tired to make love. Not that Jonathan seemed to notice that; he didn't seem to want to either.

And Jonathan, for his part, was weary and dispirited, too. Weary of the always-untidy little house, weary of the way Miranda looked these days, somehow colourless and a bit plump, weary of never having any decent clothes himself, or a break of just one night away from the kids—easily organised if only Miranda would make the effort. Weary of looking for new clients, of hopelessly following up the occasional promising lead. And too weary a lot of the time to tell Miranda he wanted her still and wanted to make love to her.

They began to quarrel, to blame one another for what was going wrong; Rosie and Daisy sat sucking their thumbs, silent, sad witnesses to the disintegration of a marriage.

They went to the Kingstons' Christmas party, and Francesca greeted them, dazzling in black satin, her blond hair a silken wave snaking down her back. Miranda tried to smile at her generously and failed, and when, later, Murray, instead of issuing his annual proposal, asked her what the matter was, she burst into tears and told him.

'Hey, hey,' he said, leading her off to the little television room. 'That's silly. You should have accepted me long ago, you see, then none of this would have happened. Anyway, he seems to be getting on rather well with Babs Hemingway. Did you see her? Scraggy blonde in scarlet silk. Just got a very expensive divorce and a house to match in Wiltshire. Wants a lot of work done on it.'

'Oh, Jonathan won't do anything as commercial as that,' said Miranda, sniffing loudly. 'And he hates smart, skinny women.'

'My darling, who knows what he'll do? Now you stay there and I'll get you a nice glass of champagne.'

It was a very nice champagne indeed, and then Murray began to dance with her and one thing led to another and he was kissing her and it was very exciting. Then she had some more champagne as he told her how sweet she was and, before she knew it, she was agreeing rather weakly to meet him for lunch the following week—but only if they could discuss a new artist of his and some paintings he might do of her children.

She had meant to phone and cancel it, but it so happened that Jonathan announced he was meeting Mrs Hemingway on the very same day to discuss some carving she wanted done. That looked like fate, so off to lunch Miranda went. And of course not one word was spoken about the paintings of the children, but a great many were spoken about how Murray adored her gentleness and her sincerity, and how his marriage was virtually over, in fact they were planning a divorce. A lot more champagne went down, and Miranda felt sparkly and pretty again, and allowed Murray to kiss her a great many times in the taxi afterwards.

And there it might have ended, had not Jonathan begun to be away rather a lot.

Babs Hemingway was a very exciting woman. She made Jonathan feel sexy and successful again; she pronounced his ideas fascinating; she said she knew someone who would love to put on his exhibition. She told him it was marvellous to talk to someone so creative, that she was lonely, that the divorce had left her demoralised and damaged, that he seemed to understand her as no man ever had before.

She told him he really was much too talented to be wasting his efforts on furniture—that he should concentrate solely on his carving.

She was very exciting in bed as well.

Miranda and Jonathan agreed, sadly but calmly, that their marriage was over.

That summer, Miranda and Murray spent three weeks sailing in the Maldives and Babs took Jonathan to her beach house in Barbados. Francesca was in LA with her new actor toy-boy.

Jonathan's exhibition opened in October at a smart Knightsbridge gallery; it was a great success, and there were several articles in the serious press proclaiming his talent. In no time every piece had a dot on it.

There was no Kingston party that Christmas; Miranda and Murray were too busy with their new marriage and their new house, which was in Chelsea and rather more stylish than the last one, and even more expensive. Miranda—slender, tanned, glowing—was amused to find herself one of the women she had once disapproved of, busy from morning to night, not only with fabric swatches, wallpaper samples and curtain styles, but also schools, staff, charity lunches and the necessity to fill her own wardrobe with clothes for the hectic social life Murray liked to lead. It was all wonderful fun, of course, and she never had been happier, but sometimes, just sometimes, she longed for a quiet evening at home, and supper for two, and a serious, proper conversation such as they never seemed to have. Such as she used to have with Jonathan. Murray never wanted to talk, and still less to listen to her. Then she remembered that life with Jonathan had been altogether too serious and proper—joyless even. The kind of pleasure she had these days had been unimaginable before.

Jonathan was working in the studio Babs had had built for him one dark day the following November when she appeared in the doorway. 'We've been asked to the Kingstons' for Christmas Eve,' she said. 'So civilised of them, don't you think?'

'Not really,' said Jonathan. 'I'd rather not go.'

'How suburban of you,' said Babs. 'Of course we must go. I'd love to see that funny little ex-wife of yours again. I hear she's done some interesting things to the house. Now, Jonathan, do get a move on with that, I've got an American arriving at the weekend and I think he'll like it.'

'But it's not going right,' said Jonathan. 'I can't rush it.'

'Darling, I don't give a toss how it's going,' said Babs, slipping out of her raincoat. 'And of course you can rush it. He's very rich, Jonathan, and I would like to think this studio could at least pay its way.'

Briefly, Jonathan cast his mind backwards to Miranda and her unswerving loyalty and sympathy;

160

then he crushed the thought hastily. Miranda had not been able to provide him with fame and neither had she ever—or not for a very long time—arrived in his studio stark naked in the middle of the afternoon or even in the morning and demanded to be made love to. And no, of course he didn't ever feel as if he had been bought (as Miranda had once, sweetly innocent, suggested). It was a superb working relationship and only a fool would have found fault with it.

They were late arriving at the Kingstons'; people were already eating supper. Babs disappeared upstairs and Jonathan was left, feeling slightly edgy, longing for a drink, when he became aware of a cloud of sexy, expensive perfume, felt a hand on his arm, and, turning, was confronted by Miranda, dazzling in red silk, hair piled high on her head, her lovely eyes warm with genuine pleasure. She reached up and kissed him; he had forgotten how gentle her mouth was, gentle and questing at the same time.

'Jonathan, how lovely to see you. Where's Babs?'

'Lost her already. You look great.'

'So do you. You never would wear a dinner jacket before.'

'Well . . . You know . . .'

She laughed. 'Yes, I do know. Come in and I'll find you some food. Murray's busy working the room.'

'And what a room,' said Jonathan, gazing with pleasure at it. So restrainedly chic, yet so unmistakably Miranda: warm, gently colourful, welcoming. 'You always did have taste, Miranda.'

'Yes, well,' she said lightly, 'it was something we shared.'

161

'Yes,' he said. 'One of the many things.'

Her large eyes, fixed on his, were thoughtful, almost sad, then suddenly amused.

'I'm sure Babs has wonderful taste,' she said.

He watched her as she moved about her guests. She had acquired an extraordinary sheen, a confidence, and was lovely: sleek, graceful, stylish. And yet, beneath it, the old Miranda: gentle, sweet, thoughtful. He hadn't realised how much he missed her.

Later, they danced. Miranda, careless with champagne, laughing at his stories of crass clients, of absurd commissions, moved increasingly closely into his arms (noting he was slimmer, more muscular, his features more sharply etched, not merely flattered by the perfectly cut dinner jacket, the carefully untidy haircut), reminded of his sexiness, his careful consideration of everything she said, enjoying the trouble he was taking with her.

'I was a pig of a husband,' he said suddenly, smiling down at her. 'A pig and a fool.'

'I was a drag of a wife,' she said, smiling back.

'And look at us now. Two of the people we used to despise.'

'Well, more fools us,' said Miranda. 'I like the new us much better. More fun; less smug.'

'Perhaps we should have lunch one day. Just for old time's sake.'

'Perhaps we should.'

*　　　*　　　*

'Of course, I'd never leave Babs,' he said, kissing her hand, stroking her cheek in the darkened corner of the dark little restaurant.

162

'And I'd never leave Murray,' she said, leaning forward, pressing her mouth gently against his.

And, at least once a week, Miranda and Jonathan would meet in the new Docklands studio he had bought, and talk about important things like art and creativity and real values, and make love rather splendidly. Then they would both go home again to their expensive houses and their glossy lives and their demanding partners who didn't always understand them . . . And all four of them lived pretty happily ever after.

A slice of Penny Vincenzi:
Articles and Interviews

GETTING OLDER

The thing is, obviously, I am ageless. Totally. Absolutely. I may in fact be a little older than I was (one has to be, of course, in order to have four grown-up daughters and four grandchildren), but I don't feel older. I have loads of energy (start the day with a 6 a.m. hike), I'm a size 10 and I wear the same sort of clothes as my daughters, give or take a smock and a footless tight or two. I can climb rocks and boogie-board with my grandchildren, and I do not, repeat not, have one of those fearsome things called a freedom pass—whether I qualify for one is another matter. So nobody could think I was any particular age at all. Only the other day, I stood in the post office helping an old lady look for her cash card. 'Empty your bag right out,' I said, 'and repack it, that's what I do. I'm always losing mine . . .'

'Well,' she said, 'and you're only a young girl.'

I left her on a bit of a high, and spent the rest of the day feeling exactly like a young girl, having some extra highlights put in my hair to complete the picture. And then it went a bit pear-shaped.

I went to the Royal Academy to see the Summer Exhibition, and stood in the queue wearing my cropped linen jeans and slash-necked T-shirt, sunglasses pushed up, Posh style, into my (highlighted) hair. 'Six pounds,' said the fresh-faced young man at the desk.

I frowned. 'Six? I thought it was eight.'

'Six,' he said patiently. 'For seniors.'

The floor heaved under my new, cool Tod's loafers. I felt a bit dizzy; swallowed hard, took a swig of my trendy bottled water. It was what you might call a moment of almost Damascene proportions. I mean, how did he know? I didn't ask for a senior ticket; I hadn't told him I qualified for one. So . . .

Reader, he knew. He looked at me and he knew. Here was a lady of clearly quite a few summers—she might be skinny, she might be sharply dressed, her lips might be glossed, but she wasn't young. Not at all; not one bit. And it showed.

But then again, last weekend I spent with a friend who I'd worked with when we were very young twenty-somethings. Our boss was a lady of legendary beauty and dynamism. 'God,' we used to say, 'she's just incredible. She wears those wonderful clothes and gives those amazing parties and knocks back the champagne and dances till dawn, and you know, she must be IN HER SIXTIES . . .'

Now here we are, and we're wearing wonderful clothes and giving parties and knocking back champagne and dancing till dawn, and it's just so, so great and such fun.

And it's actually a wonderful thing to be not quite so young—you are absolutely free again. OK, the face is a bit, well . . . etched, and the hair colour needs a lot of attention, but you know what? The world is ours. We can go to the cinema or the theatre at a moment's notice, accept invitations without a thought, stay out late, travel to wonderful places at any time, say what we like—no need to pretend to be clever/cultured/politically correct; in fact, the more incorrect the better.

Being not quite so young is permission to be outrageous. Of course you do need certain things,

168

like good health, a bit of money (although it goes much further without school fees, family holidays and mortgages) and a REALLY good sense of humour. But then actually, you need those things to enjoy being young as well.

MY SCHOOLDAYS

I was a pupil at Totnes High School in Devon—of which more later. My first school was in Parkstone in Bournemouth, and was in the same road that we lived in. I was an only child, so when I started school, I suddenly had all this company, and I positively skipped into school every day.

I remember my first day so clearly: walking down the road with my mother in my spanking new blazer and stripy tie; I thought I looked beautiful.

I was handed over to my class teacher, who was called Miss Crumpler, and she was the most wonderful teacher ever imaginable. She started every day with a story, which suited me very well, and then we would do our letters. I knew my letters before I started school, and when I volunteered this information on my first day, she gave me the most withering look imaginable before saying, 'Here, we do our letters properly.'

The school was totally progressive in its thinking: if you were good at sums, you were moved into a class with the nine-year-olds, and if you were not so good at English, you moved down to work with the younger children. Academically, I shone there, especially at English, and I was very good at writing stories. I remember one day Miss Crumpler giving us back our essays and saying to me, 'Very neatly written, Penny.' And as if that wasn't enough, she added, 'Also, I see that you know something I didn't know you knew anything about.' She paused for effect before adding, 'Inverted commas.' I felt such pride that no one else in the class knew what they were. I was excellent at mental arithmetic and times tables, too.

Miss Crumpler held sway over the class of five-year-olds—if you were naughty, she would hang you over her lap for the rest of the lesson. It was the ultimate shame. I'm sure that if she could see my handwriting now, I'd be hung over her knee all over again.

It wasn't a proper school building; it was a lovely old house with a huge garden where we were allowed to climb trees and play hide-and-seek. I walked to and from school on my own from a very young age, and one of the girls I walked with had a pony—there was a lot of competition to walk with her so you could be asked back for tea. It was an enchanted time, which made the shock of moving to Devon and starting at a new convent school when I was nine all the greater.

The new school was everything my first school wasn't. It was huge, grim and ugly, with a horrible concrete playground; it was like something out of *Jane Eyre*. My father was a banker and he worked near the school, so on the first day, he walked me there. When we approached this ugly building, the door was opened by a forbidding-looking nun wearing a full-length habit, which was utterly alien to me. I followed her in and she quickly closed the door behind me, leaving my father on the doorstep. It was like going into prison, and I remember

170

wondering whether I would ever see him again.

It was a very scary place. The nuns were terribly strict and hit the pupils on the hand with a ruler regularly. I've had four children and can't remember the pain of childbirth, but I can remember the pain of that ruler very clearly.

Another awful memory of that time was when our class teacher, Sister Luke, died of tuberculosis. It was such a shock to learn that someone I knew had died. Not being a Catholic, I didn't know the procedures at such events, but the next thing I knew, the class was filing past Sister Luke's open coffin. It was presented to us as a treat. I tried not to look, but of course I did, and I thought she looked beautiful. It was a tough thing for a little girl to have to do, but it made me aware of the reality of death from a young age.

Shortly after this, I told a nun during an RE lesson that I didn't believe that there was such a place as Hell, and her face contorted before she bellowed, 'Well, you will one day!' That, more than the picture of poor Sister Luke, has haunted me to this day, and I'm still frightened of Hell.

Thankfully, I was only there for two years before I won a place at Totnes High School, which I have very happy memories of. I continued to love English, and wrote lots of articles for the school magazine and got involved with putting on plays. I liked Latin and history, too, but was hopeless at science; by then, I'd developed the unfortunate habit of shutting off when not interested in something, and I didn't listen at all in science classes. As a result, I had very uneven report cards: glowing comments from English and history, and scathing ones from the sciences.

I spent a lot of time on the bus writing lurid love stories with another girl, every one of which contained a harrowing childbirth scene—which was all we knew about then. We both dreamed of being writers with Mills & Boon. I was chatting with friends recently, and they were all talking about how desperate they were to leave school. I was such a drip: I remember crying on my last day—I just loved school.

BEING A MOTHER

So there I stood, heart in mouth (sorry about the cliché, but that's exactly where it seemed to be), watching my daughter make a very slow, painful and brave journey from the car to the house. She'd been in hospital; I yearned to help, to call for a stretcher, carry her even, do anything that would make it easier for her. But I wasn't allowed to—she had to do it on her own.

In the end, I couldn't bear watching her any longer; I went into a corner and tried and failed not to cry, determined that she should not see me. If she could be brave, then surely so could I. Eventually she made it; we helped her into bed and she smiled up at me in triumph. I couldn't believe how dreadful it had been. I still cry thinking about it. For she is mine, part of me. If she hurts, I hurt, if she is unhappy, I am unhappy and if she triumphs, so do I.

But this is not some tousle-headed moppet of two or three, nor some fragile, vulnerable nymphet, not a small child, or even a child at all; this is a

172

grown woman with children of her own. But it doesn't make any difference—absolutely none at all . . .

So it was when she and her sister were having their babies—long, agonising hours they were, when I sat, miserably and guiltily pain-free, waiting for the phone to ring, imagining, remembering, praying. Had anyone told me when I sat up with them at night, nursing them through measles and chickenpox, changing sicky sheets and cuddling away nightmares, that I would be fretting and fussing just the same twenty years later, I would not have believed them. Nor that I would be as fiercely outraged when their hearts were broken (how dare he?), or they were rejected by some examining body (how dare it?), as when they came home crying over slights in the playground.

A mother is a mother is a mother, as Gertrude Stein might have said, and there is no moment at which the umbilical cord is ever properly cut. It tightens, it throbs, it aches; and every so often it slackens, and for a little while you think yourself free, only to feel it hauled hard upon again at each moment of need.

It is not just suffering that makes the maternal breast heave; I have friends who have endured the most appalling traumas at the hands of their children. One watched her daughter become so addicted to drugs that her own possessions were sold to fund their purchase and she didn't know for a whole year where the girl was. Not an hour of a day passed, she said, when she didn't think about that child. She felt lost herself, lost and totally bereft. She left a spare key in the official family hiding place (against all instructions from counsellors and the like), and when finally, and it seemed miraculously, the daughter reappeared, she welcomed her with an absolutely full heart.

You don't need to know all to forgive all; you just need to be a mother. Other friends, happily retired in the South of France, enjoying one another's company after raising their large family, found themselves confronted by one of their daughters, who announced that she was pregnant and that the father of the baby had left her. There was no question, she said, of having a termination; she would keep the baby and raise it on her own. I suspect you will not be surprised by what happened next; she did not raise it quite on her own but instead moved into the peaceful little French house, which became rather less peaceful and filled with nappies, bottles and colicky crying. The retirement was over before it began.

'But we had to do it,' said her mother. 'We were angry with her, of course we were, but we couldn't abandon her, or anyway, I felt we couldn't. She was so alone and helpless, and who else would have looked after her?' adding that her husband had been all for a bit of brisk abandonment, possibly agreeing to hold the baby for a few months while its mother sorted herself out. 'But she was always vulnerable, you see. Even as a child. I always had to take special care of her, more than the others. I would have felt so guilty.'

And so would I and daresay so would you. We talk big, about how they're grown up now and can take care of themselves, but we know they can't, not really: they need us still and we like it that they do. I was moved by the story of singer Pete Doherty, whose father said he would have nothing more to do with him but whose mother said she would only have treatment after finding a lump in her breast if Pete would submit himself to rehab. It seems she knew a thing or two about the umbilical cord and its permanency. Emotional blackmail you could say (and why not in such a desperate situation?), but I think there was much more to it than that. She knew she could reach out and touch him as no one else could.

I have always averred that as a mother your prime duty is to be on your child's side. Not necessarily agreeing with them, or even considering them to be in the right over every single thing (that would be very bad mothering indeed), but absolutely able to sympathise with and support them even as you argue and chastise them.

It's loyalty, I suppose you could call it, at its simplest. You are allowed to criticise and complain about your children, but let anyone else so much as give them a nasty look, or suggest in the mildest terms that perhaps they might do a little more to help, get a job or change a boyfriend (for instance) and they could be very sorry indeed. The point being that life is tough and everyone needs a refuge from it. You need at least one person to tell you that you're clever, beautiful and lovable when you get fired, or dumped, or fail an exam, even if you know in your heart of hearts that there is some slight degree of prejudice on offer.

I shall never forget failing a ballet exam when I was about nine; my mother was not so much sorry for me as outraged, and was prepared to go and argue with the very grand lady from the Royal Academy and tell her there must have been a mistake. I think I knew she was wrong and that

175

there had been absolutely nothing of the sort, but her wrath was soothing, the opposite of salt in the wound. The more so because she was prepared to go into battle for me, for she was quite shy, and I knew even then how hard it would be and how staunchly behind me therefore she must be.

There are countless stories of maternal heroism, from the more dramatic ones of women continuing with pregnancies that threaten their own lives, or rushing into blazing houses to rescue their babies, to the quieter ones of insisting on second medical opinions, of fighting for educational rights, of demanding justice against playground—and even staffroom—bullies.

Motherhood is very much about courage. It comes as a by-product of pregnancy, a sort of extra hormone; you need it not only to take you through the whole uncomfortable, bloody business of the immediate future but also to carry you through the rest of your mothering life.

MY HERO: MARJE PROOPS

It was 1962 when I went to work for Marje Proops; she was at the height of her fame. I saw her sweeping into the foyer, smiling her gap-toothed smile at everybody and usually joining us minions in the ordinary lift rather than getting into the posh executive one. She wasn't beautiful, but she had huge glamour, and counted among her friends such disparate people as Edith Sitwell and Tom Jones.

I'd been at the *Mirror* for about a year, working as a secretary, and I wanted to be a journalist with

176

my name in lights and on the side of buses, just like her.

The person I was working for was leaving and said he'd heard that Marje Proops was looking for a secretary, and why didn't I apply? I was frightfully excited and not terribly hopeful, but just to go and be interviewed by her seemed like heaven.

I went down to the editorial floor, where she had an office off the newsroom. My first impression was of an incredibly powerful personality, combined with an extraordinary niceness. She was wearing a red suit—she loved red—and a pair of wild glasses, and she smoked all the time, through a long cigarette holder. She looked vivid, vibrant, exciting; I was absolutely gobsmacked. People kept coming in to tell her jokes and gossip, and even the editor to discuss her next page, but somehow she managed to make me feel as if I was the one person in the room who really mattered.

After a while, she said, 'I think we'll suit each other very well. When can you start?' I said, 'Oh, straight away, but there is just one little thing,' and she said, 'Yeees?'—she had this lovely chuckle— and I said, 'I'm pregnant.'

Now in those days, you didn't go on working when you'd had a baby, but I intended to. She looked just a tiny bit doubtful, and I said, 'Oh it's not going to make any difference to my life' (you do really believe that first time round; I genuinely couldn't see any problems). Since she had a child of her own, she was fully aware that it might make just a little difference; it said everything about her that she took me on nonetheless.

She was so ahead of her time, doing that. And she was so good to me. My mother didn't live near

177

me, my husband, Paul, was at that point a struggling photographer, and life wasn't entirely easy. She became another mother to me; we lived in the same area, albeit at rather different ends of it, and she would take me home in her car, dropping me and the shopping off, shouting at Paul to look after me as she drove away. I wasn't very well when I was about six months pregnant, and she used to pack me off home after lunch every day, which she certainly shouldn't have done. If somebody asked where I was, she'd say, 'Oh, she's off doing a job for me.'

She knew how much I wanted to be a journalist, and she started letting me help with research and get quotes from people for her articles. It was strictly against the rules, as the *Mirror* was, like all papers, completely dominated by the unions. But she risked it, because she wanted me to have a chance.

I found out what fun journalism was, and that I did have a certain flair for it. We worked together well; she liked to sit and talk through an article as I wrote it, and I would sit by her desk and proffer the (very) occasional suggestion or go and look things up for her. No Google in those days; you had to go to the library and sit for hours, going through piles of dusty books and files. It was terribly exciting.

Her job was two-sided in those days: she wrote opinion pieces and profiles of well-known people, as well as being a fantastic agony aunt. She always attended the Labour Party Conference and was friends with many of the leading politicians. And she was passionate about her readers; she took enormous notice of everything in their letters, and there was no length she wouldn't go to if she thought one of them might be in real trouble, notifying the police if necessary, or the social services. She knew how important her relationship with them was, and she never failed them. I learnt so much working for her. She had hugely high standards; she was a perfectionist.

She even got me into the NUJ, the journalists' union, which was a big battle. But she won. She rang me at midnight at home after an endless meeting, and said, 'Darling, you're in.'

I left her with great regret after a couple of years, and moved on, but we stayed friends for the rest of her life. We went on having lunch together, telling jokes, and giggling and gossiping. I used to save up funny stories and naughty ones for her, because she loved them so much.

She endured a lot of ill-health, but she never complained, simply ignored it. She had major back surgery and was in bed, forbidden to move, for six weeks; instead of letting them put 'Marjorie Proops is ill' at the bottom of her page, she had a desk specially constructed that fitted in some way above her bed, and never missed a deadline. Her ambition was, she always said, to die at her desk, writing her column, and be found by the cleaners in the morning, and she nearly managed it: she attended the paper's conference every day when she was well into her eighties, and the day before she died, she handed the editor her column when he went to see her in hospital.

It was a piece of great good fortune, meeting her and working for her; I shall always be grateful for it. And for her.

THE EIGHTIES

I have a shameful admission: I liked the eighties. Sorry, but I did. I liked lots of things about them: their gloriously blind optimism; the sense that the streets not just of London but of just about everywhere in the country were paved with gold; that if you bought something, such as a house or shares, it would soar in value before the ink on the transaction had dried.

I liked the way we (the women among us, anyway) looked: the absurdly labelled 'power dressing', the slick suits and killer heels, the brilliant primary colours, the sharp shiny bobs. I liked the entrepreneurial spirit, and I liked the fact that the country was operating at a fast and efficient level once more after all those dismal winters of discontent.

I even quite liked yuppies, with their cheerful profligacy, spraying champagne over their Porsches and one another before settling down to another bit of multimillion-pound dealing with a tug at their red braces. They were amusing to watch; they contributed to the gaiety of the nation—although perhaps not if you were unfortunate enough to be in the same bar or restaurant as them.

Restaurants, now: they improved a lot in the eighties too. Not just famous ones, such as Carluccio's and Bibendum (which were, of course, wonderful), but just-down-the-road places where you could have a really nice meal and a bottle of wine at bearable cost. Food improved beyond all recognition, al dente veg was invented, sales of cookery books rocketed and the foodie was born. Marks & Spencer launched the chicken Kiev, to be served up unblushingly by thousands of women at dinner parties.

Health was an increasing obsession, in the form of gyms, personal trainers and aerobics classes, along with dawn jogging and the fight for a place in the London Marathon.

The supermodel was created, refusing to get out of bed for less than $10,000, personalities as much as clothes hangers; the antics of Naomi, Elle and Linda were chronicled endlessly in the gossip columns, rather as those of Paris and Posh are today. Only there was a bit more to say about them—they served considerably more purpose than simply carrying the latest handbag. And the dress designer personality was born: Karl Lagerfeld, Ralph Lauren and Giorgio Armani became as famous as their clothes.

Houses stopped being somewhere to live and became investments. Prices rose by an average of £10,000 a month as the decade wore on; a broom cupboard in Chelsea went on the market for £90,000. Thanks to Margaret Thatcher, people could buy their council houses. Estate agents became all-powerful, selling the same house four times over in as many months. People were encouraged to borrow against the rocketing value of their homes to buy yachts and Ferraris and pieces of foreign real estate; dinner-party conversations led to talk of futures and commodities and market forces (the justification for all sorts of unattractive corporate behaviour).

A popular television soap, *Dallas* and *Dynasty* apart, was *Capital City*, wonderful stuff about traders and their dizzy lifestyle; Harry Enfield created Loadsamoney, who was quite horribly recognisable.

We even had a dash of Rule Britannia in the Falklands. It was all rather exciting.

Then it all went wrong, in a great rolling tragedy on an Ancient Greek scale. It began with the great storm of 1987, when the country was stripped of many of its trees overnight and the stock market, a few days later, of much of its value. Optimism became pessimism. From the sense that anything was possible, it seemed that nothing was.

House prices crashed. The phrase 'negative equity' was coined, as huge mortgages bore no relation to property values. Market forces became rather less attractive as they led to widespread redundancies. The Porsches went, along with the champagne.

There was a parallel roller coaster, not precisely linked to the stock and property markets, but certainly encouraged by their rise and fall: Lloyd's of London, the global insurance market, had quietly been recruiting thousands more of those legendarily wealthy creatures called Names from the ranks of the not-so-rich. People yearning for the social status that Lloyd's brought—along with the seemingly unstoppable annual payouts— used equity in their property as their 'wealth'. It is only fair to say that this was against Lloyd's rules; the banks that provided letters of credit connived in the deception.

It wasn't so much the great crash that did for the Lloyd's Names; more the relentless increase in demands for money that replaced the seemingly God-given cheque: an avalanche of claims over the disease asbestosis, a few natural disasters, and rocketing risks for things such as satellites. But losses on the Stock Exchange, and in the property market, were certainly contributory factors.

The stark difference was that the demands on Lloyd's Names were infinite. The yuppies could sell their property and Porsches, draw a line and start all over again—and many did. For Lloyd's Names there was no such relief; they had signed up to an unlimited commitment. If there were insurance claims, Names had to meet them—to the grave and beyond, as one embittered soul put it to me. There were divorces, broken homes, suicides. I found it all so fascinating that I wrote a book about it . . .

HAVING IT ALL

A great American comic once said that telling your toddler he must not be jealous of a new baby because you love them both the same is rather like telling your wife she shouldn't be jealous of your mistress for the same reason.

But what do you tell the father of a screaming infant when he feels horribly rejected by his exhausted and harassed wife? What reassurance can he be given that she loves and desires him as much as ever, when the evidence of his own eyes is so obviously to the contrary?

There he is, shoved aside in the marital bed to make room for an intruder, one who, moreover, is snuggled up against your breast—where *he* likes to be—and quite probably nuzzling it as well.

He's trying to tell you about some corporate

crisis at work, and how he overcame it, and you're only—at best—half listening, or at worst actually dropping off to sleep. Meanwhile, he's busy wondering how his natty little two-door sports car was exchanged for a five-door tank filled with baby seats, mobiles and stickers. Is it any wonder that the poor chap gets a tad edgy from time to time?

I exaggerate, of course. There's no shared happiness like that created by a new baby, no greater sense of wonder; and no greater sense of achievement as the infant begins to grow, smile, walk and talk, and generally become a successful, cheerful, well-adjusted child.

I did it four times, and the sense of joy and wonder never faded. But truly, I got tired—terribly tired. And cross. And confused. And shouted a lot. My cooking—never cordon bleu anyway—took a nosedive, and the chap who delivered pizzas became a family friend.

The house was in chaos. Our social life died. And my poor husband stood right there at the back of the queue, waiting (mostly) patiently for a few exhausted minutes when he could have a scrap of attention from me. Inevitably he too got cross sometimes and shouted as well.

And here lies the crux of a thorny question married women have faced since time immemorial: is it possible to be the Perfect Wife while you're trying to be the Perfect Mother?

The fact is that when children arrive, women turn away from the husbands who have up to that point been the focus of all their nurturing and love and passion.

The trouble is that children are more rewarding for women than they are for men. I'm sorry, the

184

feminists can howl as loudly as they like, but it's true. Women usually want babies more than men do. We find them a more irresistible prospect (I think it's called biology).

We (usually) get more excited at the first smile, the first tooth, the first toddle. We (usually) cope better with the boredom, the mess, the racket; and we (usually) find the inevitable loss of income, freedom and time for ourselves easier to contemplate.

It does help *hugely*, of course, if the father enjoys it all too, in a sufficiently mature and selfless way, and not just from a practical point of view.

But fathers are born, not made, in my experience, and for every caring, sharing chap, showing pictures of the latest scan in the pub and earnestly sourcing organic carrots for the purée, there are a whole lot more feeling rejected and put upon and wondering where on earth the girl they married went to.

Men love to be mothered and fed and watered like they were when they were little—and when their wife finds a real child who needs mothering, the result can be dreadful tension in the marriage.

For the woman, the demands of children are immediate and constant, and press all the right buttons—the ones marked 'urgent'. No one except a monster—or a mother from the fifties, but we'll come on to her in a minute—could ignore a hungry baby, a whining toddler or a sick child.

The demands of a husband, meanwhile, also press emotional buttons in a wife, but in stark contrast; you can respond with 'in a minute', 'not now' or even 'for goodness' sake, can't you see I've got enough to cope with?' Which, of course, you

185

have. The point is that every mother wants to be a Perfect Mother. You wouldn't set out on the whole baby business if you didn't.

It's the holy grail, the fallacy peddled by all those baby books and magazine and newspaper articles—for many modern women it has become more important than having a good career; indeed it is a career in itself. And if you fail at motherhood, having set out to create a domestic dream, you feel pretty damn bad about yourself.

At the beginning, you see yourself as calm, smiling, loving, with lots of time to develop talents and interests, read stories and bake organic bread. You may well achieve something pretty close to that.

Personally, I seemed to be stressed, scowling and always rushing out to the corner shop to buy a packet of sliced white. But the problem is that trying to be a perfect mother takes an inordinate amount of time. And energy.

Just creating the requisite atmosphere for bedtime—everyone settled into freshly laundered beds and cots while you read them stories, rather like a scene from the White Company catalogue—requires more advance planning and critical analysis than the invasion of a small country, or the running of a large company.

As for your own bedtime (and your husband's, which is unlikely to come at the same time), it takes place somewhere between ten and the small hours, after you've filled the lunch boxes, sorted the socks and done a bit of frantic ironing.

Even then, as you climb exhausted into bed, your sleep is frequently interrupted by cries of 'Mummy, I feel sick/had a bad dream/can't find teddy.'

That's when the prospect of sex with your husband becomes something of a distant dream.

And if you have to add into that equation going out to work, delivering and fetching children from the nursery or child minder, and then embarking on the chores and the cooking when you finally get home, you end up running on empty pretty quickly.

Soon, you realise you've come a long way from that person you set out to be years before, when you swanned up the aisle full of aspirations for an idyllic life with your man: the Perfect Wife. Or at least the Very Good Wife.

Now, obviously one man's 'very good wife' is not necessarily exactly like another's; not all men want the Jerry Hall ideal of maid in the living room, cook in the kitchen and whore in the bedroom— although I can't personally think of many who don't, not if they were being honest.

The Very Good Wife is life-enhancing. She makes things fun. She's the independent, spirited woman her husband fell in love with and wanted to marry.

But enter one small, noisy, completely exhausting stranger, possessed of such monumental selfishness and manipulative powers and capable of creating chaos on so unimaginable a scale if it doesn't get exactly what it wants, and with the very best will in the world, the Very Good Wife becomes a terrible one, lost in exhaustion and utterly preoccupied with her child.

Of course it was not always like this. My mother's generation—who ran their families in the forties and fifties—always put their husbands first.

The children were in bed when the householder's key turned in the lock, a delicious supper was

187

waiting in the oven, and mother became wife, in a freshly laundered something, a smile on her face and a patient ear at the ready for the recounting of the trials of the day.

At the weekend, what Father said went; the family scuttled to do his bidding, or at least what he wanted, and anyway, he'd probably be out a lot of the time playing golf, or going to the football.

Presumably children must still have had bad dreams or felt sick, but they knew that once Daddy was home, he was the most important person. This lofty figure took a tumble in the sixties, when mothers began to go out to work.

But a man's needs were still out there in the forefront. Even the divine Shirley Conran, High Priestess of Getting It All Done Somehow, counselled that we should make sure that he always had a freshly ironed shirt at the ready. And a handkerchief too. However long and hard the female day—and even though he was expected to help—he only helped in small proportions. And when push came to shove, he was still the most important person.

This inevitably bred resentment in the house. That, I think, was the point at which we women began to realise there was a genuine battle raging in the home—tearing us in two as we sought to devote ourselves to our husband and children in equal measure.

And since by then many of us had gone out to work, trying to be a perfect mother and a perfect wife—while consumed with guilt at leaving our babies at home—was inevitably doomed to failure.

These days, men are beginning to understand that when offspring arrive, the paternal figure is no longer going to retain the unquestioning devotion of his wife. Fathers know that families are a shared responsibility which they've created, and they do an enormous amount to help.

I look at them in awe as they walk around Sainsbury's on Saturday mornings, patiently checking their lists, babies strapped to their chests while toddlers run riot.

One of the main reasons for this is that their wives have probably just worked a sixty-hour week in a high-powered job, and the man is sensible enough to know that if he demands his dinner on the table at 6 p.m., he's likely to get a ready meal tipped all over his head as his wife dashes past with a dirty-nappy bin under her arm.

The bottom line is that it's jolly tough on a relationship not having any time or energy left over for each other.

Communication might not quite break down, but it starts to crumble. It leads, inevitably, to a sense of huge frustration and questions of how and why did we ever get into this. And I don't know what the answer is.

Maybe the best solution is to effectively put the marriage on hold: to recognise the problem and know that time—and the arrival of the youngest child at school age—will to a large extent solve it.

I would not wish to imply that that is the end of one's parental headache—there are positive migraines in store in the form of education, adolescence and God knows what else—but at least there's a bit more time for a couple to rediscover one another, and to remind themselves that you can have sex without a baby screaming in the other room.

The other way to attempt to solve this intractable problem is for women to temper their ambitions a bit: to accept that there's no such thing as a perfect anything, that striving for it is counterproductive, and that good old muddling along—giving your husband and children as much time as you can—often works better, and is actually more fun.

MY CAREER IN A NUTSHELL

I always wanted to write. I started with rip-off Enid Blytons, then at nine I wrote my own magazine called *Stories* and took it to school to flog, without success. By the time I was sixteen, I wanted to be a journalist. I wrote for the parish magazine, but was fired for being disrespectful to the ladies' sewing circle. I wrote something flippant and they complained to the vicar. I didn't go to university; I left school after A levels, having suddenly decided that I should get on and be a journalist. I then went to a smart secretarial college in London.

My first real job was as a junior secretary at *Vogue*. It was a very snooty place; I was an unsophisticated, badly dressed nineteen-year-old, while everyone in the office wore hats all the time. But I did get a terrific feel for how to put a magazine together, doing it physically with paper and glue.

I began to work my way up. I was very good at having ideas, I was mustard keen and I would do anything. I became a secretary to the editor at *Tatler*, and he took me with him when he moved to the *Daily Mirror*. I worked as a fashion and beauty editor at magazines such as *Woman's Own*, before becoming a contributing editor for *Cosmopolitan*.

A career change presented itself in the 1980s. It was the golden age of the sex-and-shopping novel, and women like me in journalism were being signed up to write huge blockbusters about glossy lifestyles. I had a good idea for a book, so I got an agent, wrote a synopsis and sample chapters, and sold it to Century Hutchinson. I suppose I first realised I could make a real living out of it the day I got in the *Sunday Times* top ten with my first book. I thought gosh, that can't be true, it can't be me. Even now, with every book I write, I get more frightened about how it will do. I can't even eat.

My tip for any aspiring novelist would be to go out and buy a biro and a pad of paper and sit down and start. You don't need a lot of time, or a fancy word processor. People have a romantic view that writers wait for inspiration, which is a load of old toot. You get an idea and then you work like a demon. When you're ready to send a book out, get yourself a really good agent. They know all the editors and you're less likely to end up on the slush pile.

My heroes are the great editors like Paul Dacre, Harold Evans and Anna Wintour, storytellers like Jilly Cooper, and politicians like Lord Carrington and Margaret Thatcher. I also greatly admire the Queen. These people have always inspired me, but I suppose my motivation, the thing that drives me to sit down and write each day, is seeing my books published. If no one would publish me, I would probably stop.

Q & A

Where do you get the ideas for your novels?
From talking to people. Often during end-of-dinner-party conversations. They're what I call 'touch-points' or 'what-ifs'. 'What if your husband asked you to commit perjury to keep him out of jail?' or 'What if you discovered your mother had abandoned you as a baby?'

Do you have a special writing retreat?
Not really. Having trained on the *Daily Mirror*, I could write on the London Underground. I have a cottage in Wales where I do everything that I do in London, so I work there, have people to dinner and the grandchildren to stay. It's neither a retreat nor an inspiration, but a second home.

Do you treat yourself when you've finished?
When I've written the final sentence of the book I've been working on, it feels amazing. I actually type 'The End' and always have a glass of champagne, whatever time of day it is. I feel I could fly, walk on water. Then about three days later I get postnatal depression and start missing all the characters and mope about waiting to hear from my editor so at least I can talk about them.

Have you ever had to worry about money?
God, yes. Before I became a novelist, my husband and I published a fashion and beauty magazine. I gave up my job and we traded down our house and plunged the capital into the magazine. Then our

backer changed the terms of the deal three days before we published. We'd gone too far to pull out, so our lawyer agreed to underwrite a loan from the bank. We were warned what to do if the bailiffs came, but amazingly it was a success. For a time it was nerve-racking, though.

What is your biggest extravagance?
Flying club class, because it makes travelling so much nicer. And it's lovely to be able to help the children when they need it. My other main extravagance is clothes—I have learned to love shopping.

You're incredibly stylish—do you ever not make an effort?
Every day? I slob around in trackie bums and trainers and I look awful every day for most of the day. I just scrub up well when I have to.

There's a ten-year age gap between your two oldest daughters and your two youngest. How did you divide your time between them?
The age gap was actually a huge help. Just as I had two stroppy teenagers to deal with, I had two dear little cuddly babies. And the boringness of the babyhood was greatly eased by the thought that Polly or Sophie was about to be home soon to talk to.

Do you see them often?
Yes, usually every week, and we email and phone each other constantly.

How do you celebrate your birthday?
I am very childish about it. It usually coincides with Easter, and everyone comes to our house in Wales. We have a ritual where, after an Easter egg hunt, we have presents before lunch and champagne, so by the time I sit down to lunch I'm drunk already! One of my sons-in-law, Simon, cooks lunch, and he and Sophie and their children make me a cake. I look forward to it all year.

What do you never leave home without?
Even just to walk the dog at 6.30 in the morning, I wouldn't go anywhere without my credit cards, glasses and phone. If I'm going anywhere remotely important, I always take my styling tongs. I have the most hideously difficult hair in the world. The slightest hint of damp in the air leaves it limp, lank and unflattering.

What part of the world are you happiest in?
The Gower peninsula in Wales, where I have the cottage. The sea meets the sky there, the weather is surprisingly wonderful, the people are gentle and friendly. Wild ponies wander along the roads, lambs trail after their mothers just about everywhere, including your garden, and my heart lifts just thinking about it.

What or who makes you laugh?
My daughters, my grandchildren when they tell me jokes, Morecambe and Wise, *The Good Life* and Rory Bremner. Listening to *The News Quiz* on Radio 4 and watching *Have I Got News For You* makes me helpless with laughter.

What's your pet peeve?
Horrid words like 'diarise' and 'incentivise' and absurd phrases such as 'accessing the workplace'. What's wrong with 'looking for a job'?

What would be your dream holiday?
My dream would be to go to the Galapagos Islands. Not a holiday in the strict sense, because it's uncomfortable, hot and very hard work. But the thought of seeing those creatures, the seals, giant tortoises and turtles, and amazing birds like the albatross, and following in Darwin's footsteps is totally exciting.

Who's your favourite male and female film star of all time?
James Stewart is my favourite male film star. He had a wonderful voice, and that slightly puzzled look. Ginger Rogers is my favourite female star. I could watch her dance for ever. She seemed literally to float above the ground; your heart dances with her.

What is your favourite feel-good film?
Notting Hill. Marvellous characters, brilliant script, perfect performances, great music, total charm. Love it.

What is your favourite word?
'Wonderful'. It's evocative, and you can't say it and sound anything but happy.

As dictator for the day, what law would you make?
I would make a law that everyone should listen more. I mean *really* listen, carefully and properly,

and at every level—from the politicians upwards and downwards. It would do wonderful things for world peace, for society and for family life.

What is your favourite scent?
Chanel No. 5.

What single earthly pleasure would you most miss?
Champagne. It does so much more than simply top up your alcohol levels. It truly lifts the spirits, makes a grey day blue. All that sort of stuff.

A DAY IN MY LIFE

A writer's working day, it seems to me, is rather less interesting than watching paint dry. You sit down, you write; several hours later you stop writing and stand up again.

But then I am a writer, and of course there is a little more to it than that. My favourite reading matter in the entire week is 'A Life in the Day Of' in the *Sunday Times*, when I sit entranced, discovering what time an actress gets up, as opposed to an architect or a political activist, and what they all have for breakfast, and whether they work better before or after lunch, and of course that's the point: I am familiar with my day and not at all with theirs. So all right, I'll try and make mine sound a little more interesting and tell you how it goes.

Actually there are three variations on my working day; the first, the most typical, is the least interesting.

I get up early; I'm very lucky in that the moment I wake up, my mind is clear and busy and I can, if under huge pressure, pull on a sweater and some trackie bums and go straight into my study and my story, having first made a mug of tea. But that is quite unusual; what I like to do is go for a walk, absolutely first thing, at about half past six or earlier, and yes, in the dark if it's winter, taking the dog with me. I actually start working then; it's when I do my plotting. I take my characters with me (along with the dog), mull over what they were all doing yesterday and then think very hard about what they might do today. It's an invaluable time, and I have been known to hide in a bush rather than find myself involved in conversation with someone. It's not that I'm antisocial; I love being involved in conversation but not on my plotting walk. Actually most of the other dog-walkers know of my strange behaviour and say, 'I won't disturb you, I know you're working' as I stomp along.

When I get back, I have a shower, change into something slightly less muddy and wet, load up the dishwasher and head for my study. The first task in there is clearing my desk from the day before; I leave it in total chaos when I finish in the evening, books open, paper piled high, files spilling all over the place. Sorting it out sorts my head out too. I look at my emails but try to ignore them unless they're really urgent, and then open up the current book on my laptop.

For at least an hour, sometimes much longer, I edit what I wrote the day before: cut—or lengthen—conversations, carve up descriptive passages, flesh out characters (a very short sentence can often do this; learning that someone is terrified

197

of spiders or loves Mozart can make an enormous difference to a reader's perception of and sympathy with them). Then I start writing again. Sometimes this is a very fast process—I have been known to write four thousand words in a day—other times a slower one. Neither of which means very much: some chapters or passages require careful attention and much deliberation, others a fast-moving description of meetings or events. Sometimes, yes, I do find it hard to write at all, but the only answer to that in my experience is to carry on sitting there and struggling. You can't run away from it; nothing ever got written by an absentee author. It's the seat of the pants on the seat of the chair, as Bernard Shaw put it, and the longer the two stay together, the more gets done.

I usually take half an hour around eleven or twelve to have my breakfast. Odd timing, but it suits me; I like to be starving, and I'm not at seven or eight in the morning. By three or four, though, I'm written out, so then I have some lunch (I know, I know, even odder) and then go into admin. Writing emails, paying bills, sorting out my diary (it's very complicated, what with professional, personal and family life) and typing up research. I do a lot of research and there's always a queue of interviews with people on the recorder to be turned into notes. At seven I stop and listen to *The Archers*.

The major variation on this comes on the days I do the research. Because I don't like using the internet—except to check things; I like it all to be original—I go to enormous lengths to find real people with experience of the world I'm writing about, and get them to talk. Usually they're very happy to do this, which is lucky for me. For *The*

Decision, for instance, I spent many hours with a divorce lawyer (the book is about a custody battle); for *The Best of Times*, which is about a motorway crash, with a traffic cop. People's generosity with their time really is amazing. Or I'll go to some disused racing track like Brooklands or long-abandoned army barracks for the atmosphere. Occasionally I go out of the country to research locations or to find people who lived in Paris during World War Two (I did!) or who were socialites in Milan in the 1960s. My next book, which is set in the cosmetic industry, has involved long sessions with perfumiers, PRs and advertising agencies. And so it goes on. It's always fascinating and I love it.

So that's another sort of day in my life.

The third is when I've got a new book out and I'm hurtling around giving interviews, attending parties and festivals, signing endless copies until my writing resembles unravelled knitting, and even popping over to Ireland or the States. But that only lasts for a very few weeks and is so untypical it's hardly worth mentioning.

And now, if you'll excuse me, I must tidy my desk and start the real work of the day . . .

MY FAVOURITE BOOKS

I Wrote a Pony Book by Christine Pullein-Thompson
Aged eleven, I was jointly in love with ponies and writing, and this story about a little girl who wrote—guess what!—a pony book really inspired me. My own first 'book', written on my mother's typewriter, was a dreadful rip-off of this one.

Rebecca by Daphne Du Maurier
Haunting and beautiful, it is just perfectly written, and however many times I read it (which is about once a year!), it always casts a new spell. I fell in love with Maxim de Winter, the arrogant, desperately unhappy hero, Mrs de Winter, his second, adoring, hapless wife, and Rebecca, the gloriously wicked haunting heroine, and have carried them round in my head ever since! A huge influence in my own writing.

The Pursuit of Love by Nancy Mitford
It sounds odd, but this book was one of the things that really inspired me to have a big family. The sense of fun and jokes and closeness and loyalty at its heart is irresistible.

America's Queen by Sarah Bradford
I've always been fascinated by Jacqueline Kennedy Onassis, but this book is a breathtaking study in courage—one of the most important qualities a person can have.

Gone with the Wind by Margaret Mitchell
Literally life-changing. I read it in about three days (and, under the covers by torchlight, three nights) and realised that writing something this gripping and sweeping was what I wanted to do. I'm still trying!

Just William by Richmal Crompton
And all the other William books—each one is a small gem. Not only laugh-out-loud funny, but incredibly clever in terms of plot and character creation. Who could ever forget William, or indeed

200

Violet Elizabeth?

Brideshead Revisted by Evelyn Waugh
Probably the most exquisite book ever written. It's about everything really: God, sex, family, the power of beauty to beguile—all with a terrible vein of sadness running through it.

Jane Eyre by Charlotte Brontë
Who could resist this one? This wonderful, wild, romantic story of the plain but clever governess and the arrogantly mysterious Mr Rochester who falls in love with her, and she with him, of course. Me too, indeed, for who could resist his brooding sexuality? Mr Rochester was the second man I fell in love with (after Rhett Butler), remaining faithful to him even after I discovered his bigamous intentions, and knowing I would not, like the virtuous Jane, have walked from his arms and his house and on to the wild moor, facing a future without him. Never did a heroine deserve her happy ending more.

READ ON FOR A SNEAK PREVIEW OF PENNY'S NEW NOVEL . . .

Love at first sight, that was what it was; heady, life-changing, heart-stopping stuff. It had happened to her only twice before, this sense of recognition, of something so absolutely right, right for her and what she was and what she wanted to do and be. She hadn't hesitated, hadn't played any silly games, hadn't said maybe or I'll think about it or I'll let you know, just yes, of course, of course she'd like to do it very much, and then looked at her watch and seen she was already late for her board meeting, and after the briefest farewell had left the restaurant.

The first thing she did, back in the taxi, was call her husband. She always did that. He needed to know, and she needed him to know; he was so very much part of it all, his life hugely affected as well as hers. He had been pleased, as she had known he would be, said he would look forward to discussing it over dinner. Only of course she was going to be late for dinner now, which she reminded him of, and he only sighed very lightly before saying well, he'd look forward to seeing her whenever it was.

He really was a truly accommodating man, she thought. She was very lucky.

*   *   *

'Well, that was very satisfactory.' Hugh Bradford sat back in his chair and ordered a brandy. He never drank at lunchtime normally; had gone through the whole meal on water and one modest glass of champagne to seal the deal. He'd have liked to; he really envied the Mad Men generation, with their Martini-fuelled lifestyle, and had thought more than once that the superb beef Wellington he was eating really did deserve better than Evian to wash it down. But there it was: life was different now, and it was certainly impossible to imagine Bianca Bailey allowing even the smallest sip of alcohol— well, she'd had a couple of sips of champagne, but he could feel her reluctance—to blur the clear-blue-sky clarity of her brain.

He wondered—briefly and inevitably, perhaps, for she was very attractive—if she ever surrendered control; whether in flagrante at least she might lose herself—and then returned to the present. Such meanderings had no place in the here and now, or even the future of his relationship and those of his colleagues with Bianca.

'Yes, it was excellent. I thought she would, but you never quite know . . . Yes, thanks . . .' Mike Russell, colleague of many years, nodded assent to the brandy bottle. 'Now all we've got to do is sell her to the family.'

'The family don't have any choice,' said Bradford, 'but I think they'll like her. Or at least the idea of her. Better than some man, or so they'll think. Best fix a meeting PDQ. Early next week?'

'Yes, sure. Or later this. There really is very little time.'

'I'll get Anna to sort it.'

*   *   *

'I'm going to meet the family and board of Farrells on Friday,' said Bianca to her husband. 'Friday

203

afternoon. I can't wait. It's a fantastic set-up, Henry, straight out of fiction. Or even Hollywood.'

'Really?'

'Yes. There's a matriarch, of course—there's always a matriarch in the cosmetic business.'

'Really?' said Henry again.

'Well, yes. Just think. Elizabeth Arden, Estée Lauder, Helena Rubinstein . . .'

'I'm not sure that any reflection on the cosmetic industry on my part would be very rewarding,' said Henry. 'It's not a business I know a lot about, at the moment. On the other hand, I suspect I'm about to.'

'You could be. It's an industry you have to live and breathe, just to understand it. Anyway, she— the matriarch, Lady Farrell—founded it in 1953, with her husband, who died five years ago—sad; apparently it was a great love match, lasted nearly sixty years—and then there's a daughter and a son on the board; not up to much as far as we can make out.'

'My word. A completely family affair.'

'Well, they hold all the shares at the moment. A few other mediocre people in theory help run it, or rather ruin it—it's all absolutely fascinating stuff. She's not giving in without a fight, Lady Farrell, but I think she's finally got to. The bank are about to pull the plug; hideously in debt, they are. Anyway, I—well we, Hugh, Mike and I—think there is some magic there. I can't wait to get to work on it. Going to be a long meeting, that's for sure. That OK?'

'Of course. I'm taking the children to see the Tintin film. You said you didn't want to go . . .'

'I don't,' said Bianca. 'Can't think of anything worse.'

'That's all right then,' said Henry Bailey lightly.

*   *   *

Bianca Bailey was, in business parlance, a rock star. The stage on which she performed was not the O2 Arena, or even Wembley, but the platform of high finance, and her success was measured not in terms of ticket sales or even position in the charts, but balance sheets and company flotations. A high-flying, high-profile figure, a female Midas, with a dazzling record in turning businesses around, she was at thirty-eight quite a young rock star; she was also a gift to whatever publicity people she was working with at the time, being extremely attractive: tall (five foot ten in her stockinged feet), slim, stylish, and if not quite beautiful, very photogenic and telegenic, with her mass of dark hair and large grey eyes. She was also articulate—an automatic go-to when anyone wanted a quote on some deal or buyout, when related to women at least—and charming. She was happily married (to Henry Bailey), had three delightful children, lived in a stunning, much photographed house in Hampstead and almost inevitably a very pretty country house as well, which she persisted in labelling rather inaccurately a cottage, in Oxfordshire.

Bianca had been wondering what to do next, having been a crucial part of the very successful sale of the company of which she was currently CEO—a hitherto low-visibility, almost down-market toiletry brand—when Mike Russell of Porter Bingham, a private equity firm, had called her to ask if she would like to come in for a coffee and a chat. She knew what that meant, and they knew she knew;

they had teamed up before. They had a challenge for her in the form of another unsuccessful company that needed her considerable powers.

The prospect they had laid before her was daunting. Bianca liked daunting; indeed, she found it irresistible.

'They came to us,' Mike Russell had said. 'Well, the son did. Bertram, he's called, looks like a Bertram too; nice enough chap but a bit of an idiot. They're currently losing five million a year, and frankly, we think we could do something with them. Situation's pretty dire; they're flailing around, don't know what they're doing financially at all. But there's a load of potential, especially with you on board, probably with a view to selling the company in five to eight years' time. Anyway, have a look at it, the whole thing and the figures, see what you think.'

Bianca had looked, shuddered at the figures and the state of the brand, saw what they meant about the potential, and the result had been the lunch at Le Caprice and the agreement between her and Porter Bingham to take things further towards an investment in Farrells.

'I think it's possible to turn that five million loss into a ten-million-pound annual profit in five years' time. I'd say you'll have to make an overall investment of around ten million and a further two or three million to fund the development work, but yes, I think it can be done.'

She'd smiled at them: her wide, Julia Roberts-style smile. She liked them both, which was important; they were straightforward, decisive and could be great fun. And Hugh particularly was extremely good-looking, in a conventional,

Establishment way. She often thought it was as well he wasn't her type, or she might occasionally make some less than completely professional decisions. While knowing that actually she would never do that. In her glossily successful life, she had never been swayed for an instant by personal considerations. It was one of the many reasons for her success.

*   *   *

'I'm really excited about this,' she said to Henry, when she got home after that first meeting, 'but I'd like your agreement. It's going to be tough, tougher even than the last one. What would you say to that?'

Henry said that if she really wanted to do it, then of course she must, resisting the temptation to ask her what she would do if he withheld his agreement. Bianca did what she wanted; that was what she was about. Anything else was just so much window-dressing.

He knew what lay ahead of him; as with any new project of Bianca's—and he had lived through a few in the course of their relationship—there would be a lot of lonely evenings, a commitment from her that amounted almost to an obsession, and a feeling quite often that the company under her command was situated if not actually in the marital bed, then certainly at the family table. He put up with it for two reasons: he found it quite interesting himself, observing it as he did from as dispassionate a vantage point as he could manage; and he loved Bianca as much as he admired her, and wanted her to do what made her happy. It required some unselfishness on his part; but on the other hand, it allowed him to do whatever he wanted—like buying paintings, and owning a couple of expensive pieces of horseflesh—without too much interference from anyone else.

He was not greatly given to tortured introspection—he was an only child, with all the self-confidence that condition trailed in its wake. 'We're not like other people,' he would say, and it was true.

Bianca had no siblings either: they often, in the early days of their relationship, discussed this and the bond it created between them. Indeed, she produced some statistic—she was very fond of statistics—that onlies were drawn to other onlies—'or eldests, much the same really'. The statistic went on to say that only children were proven to be highly successful and driven. Henry was not sure that this could possibly apply to him, but he was flattered by the observation and kept his counsel. The last thing he wanted was for the dynamic Bianca to regard him as some kind of amiable low achiever. Or indeed her father, the distinguished and highly esteemed historian Gerald Wood. Henry sometimes wondered if Gerald actually knew that any of them existed, so immersed was he in medieval constitution and literature, always far more immediate to him than the twenty-first century, and more so than ever since Pattie, his beloved and long-suffering wife, had died when Bianca was only nineteen.

*   *   *

'Hello, Mr Bailey. Good day?'

'Yes, not bad, thanks. You?' He wasn't going to tell the housekeeper—in front of his son—that he'd been so bored, he'd actually dropped off in his office after lunch.

'Very good, thank you. I've done the menu for the dinner party for tomorrow week if you'd like to look at it, so you can order the wine.'

'Oh—thanks. I'll take it up to my study.'

'And I've made a bolognese sauce for tonight—Mrs Bailey won't be home, you said . . .'

'No, she's got some big meeting tomorrow, so she'll be working very late. I'll eat with the children in about—oh, half an hour? But I'll cook the spaghetti, don't worry about that.'

'Right. Well, I'll just make a salad and then I'll be on my way. Ruby's in bed. Rachel's reading to her now, and then she's off; hope that's OK.'

Rachel was the nanny; no longer strictly essential, but Ruby was only eight, and some one-on-one care was still necessary. Rachel came in after school until Ruby was in bed and full-time in the holidays; a job, as she often remarked to fellow nannies on her social circuit, of unbelievable cushiness.

'Fine. Thank you, Sonia. Oh, hi, Milly, how was your day?'

'Cool.'

'That's all right, then.'

'And how was yours?'

'Oh, pretty hot.'

She reached up to kiss him.

'You're so funny.'

'I try. Done your homework?'

'Of course!'

'Sure?'

'Daddy! Don't be horrid.'

'She has done it, Mr Bailey,' said Sonia, smiling at Milly. 'She started as soon as she got in from school.'

'See! Thank you, Sonia.'

'What about your clarinet practice?'

'Done that too.'

'You're too good to be true, aren't you?'

'Absolutely I am.'

'Right. Where's Fergie?'

'Playing on the Wii.'

'Tut tut. Not allowed before seven.'

'Daddy! You sound like Mummy. See you later.'

She wandered off, her attention entirely on her phone, her fingers flying over the keys. Henry smiled indulgently at her back. Emily, nicknamed Milly at birth, was, at almost thirteen, a golden child: tall, slender, with long straight dark hair and large brown eyes. Not yet tarnished by adolescence, she was sweetly bright and charming, affectionate, chatty and extremely popular—one of the girls everyone wanted at their parties and sleepovers. In her second year at St Catherine's, Chelsea, a new and fiercely academic girls' day school, currently giving both St Paul's and Godolphin a run for their money, she was a talented musician—Grade 5 on the clarinet, on which she could also turn in a mean jazz set. Her only failure was games, at which she was a complete duffer. If a ball could be dropped, or a goal missed, Milly would drop or miss it, her only prowess being for running, at which she excelled. To her father's disappointment, she didn't even like riding very much; she found horses frightening, and had nightmares about being bolted with, but she persevered because she adored her father—and besides, her younger brother rode superbly. Indeed, several red rosettes won at local gymkhanas adorned the lavatory of the country house. Milly couldn't compete with that, but the fact that she could go out hacking beside her father meant she wasn't excluded entirely from his weekend world.

At eleven, Fergie was as good at games as Milly was bad, in every first team at his prep school, and inclined therefore to neglect academic work almost entirely. Being clever, he usually passed exams by the skin of his teeth, but Henry's early hopes of Winchester for him had long been filed under Z, as one of Bianca's favourite expressions would term it. He had the family charm and looks, though, and it was generally agreed that even if he went to a sink comprehensive, he would survive and moreover do well. Henry hoped for better than the sink comp; he thought he would at least like Fergie to pass his Common Entrance.

*   *   *

Henry went up to his study. It was on the first floor of the house—substantial detached Hampstead Victorian—and looked over the sizeable garden. He loved the house; as a child, he had lived in a similar one only two streets away. The extremely large deposit had been a wedding present from his father; people always said that that simple fact told you almost everything you needed to know about the Bailey family: that it was rich, happy, close and generous.

Hugh Bailey had been a stockbroker in the golden age of the City; he had made a fortune, retired early in 1985—'just before Big Bang, thank God', he often said—and moved his young family into a large house with a considerable amount of land and some stables, where he indulged in the life of a country gentleman, became a very good shot, and in his spare time turned his life-long hobby of antique dealing into a half-day job, as he put it. It did not greatly add to his fortune, but it did not diminish it either, and he pursued it with his charming wife, Wendy. Their two sons were sent to school at Marlborough, and their daughter went to St Mary's, Calne, along with a lot of other smart little girls.

Henry had left Oxford with a respectable 2:1 in economics, with no very clear idea of what he wanted to do. He worked for a management consultancy for a couple of years and found it very frustrating—'probably because I'm not very good at it,' he said cheerfully to anyone who asked him—so it was suggested that he join his uncle Ralph's chartered accountancy firm, based in the Strand. Here he was given a very nice office, earned an excellent salary, and was greatly liked by the staff and his clients alike; he did well, being charming, and equable as well as clever, but he would probably have left after another couple of years (finding the work at best uninspiring and at worst boring) had he not met and fallen in love with Bianca Wood, and decided within a very short time that he wanted to marry her.

In Henry's world, you didn't propose to a girl unless you could offer her a proper set-up, which translated as a nice house in a good area, and a handsome salary to support her should she wish not to work, or when she had children. He wasn't miserable at Bailey, Cotton and Bailey; he was just not very excited by the work. Which was not sufficient reason to keep him from proposing to Bianca in 1997 and marrying her in 1998.

He had met her at a dinner in the City and been immediately enchanted by her; she was sparkly and articulate, and clearly found him interesting too. She was, she said, a marketing manager at a toiletries company: 'toothpaste and deodorant, might not sound very exciting, but last year it was washing powder, so big improvement. And anyway, of course, it's not the product, it's what you can do with it. Sending the sales graph in the right direction: hard to beat.'

He asked her out to dinner that weekend; they talked for so long that the waiters were piling chairs on to tables before they realised how late it was. She invited him out the next Friday. 'My treat this time. No, that's how I operate; sorry, don't like spongers.'

Henry found watching her sign the credit card slip extremely painful, and said so; she replied that he was clearly very old-fashioned: 'Most of the men I know would be thrilled.' In the event, any discomfiture on Henry's part didn't last very long, because within three months they had moved in together.

By the time they were married in 1998, Bianca had moved jobs twice and become marketing manager of an interior design company. She continued to work until the week before Milly was born, and was back at her desk within four months, and when Fergie arrived two years later, she only stayed at home for twelve weeks. There was the nanny, she said, and she got very bored

213

rocking cradles. Which did not mean she was a bad mother; she was intensely loving and passionately involved with her children. She just operated better maternally if she had something else to do. When Ruby made her embryonic presence felt, two years after Fergie, unplanned and the result of a bout of bronchitis, a strong antibiotic and thus a decrease in the effectiveness of the pill, she did not, as some women in her position might have done, opt for a termination, just welcomed the situation a little wearily and said she liked to keep busy. Which she did. Her career trajectory had been impressive. Henry, while being immensely proud of her, and encouraging her 'every inch of the way; I know about being a new man', couldn't help wishing she would take more time off when she had the children, but they certainly didn't seem to have suffered: they were all bright and charming and self-confident. He sometimes felt also that Bianca might take a little more interest in him and his work; but then, as he so frequently said, there wasn't anything much to take an interest in. He was a partner now, he was extremely well-paid, his hours were civilised—which was more than could be said for Bianca's—and on the whole he didn't mind being the ballast in their household, as he put it. He was exceptionally good-natured. When Milly was five, Bianca was made sales and marketing director of a fabric company; that was when her salary overtook Henry's. Henry did mind that, quite a lot. Bianca teased him about it rather as she had when she paid for their second dinner together: 'Darling! It's our money, just as yours is; it pays for our family, our life. What do the proportions matter?'

He once asked her, when he had had a great deal to drink, if she would give up her job if he really wanted her to; she leaned across the table and said, 'Darling, of course, if you really wanted it, but you wouldn't, would you? You're not like that, and that's why I love you.'

And she did: very much. As indeed Henry loved her; he said, frequently, that he had been born under a lucky star. And from time to time, when life was a little less than perfect, he would remind himself that a bit of boredom at the office and an occasional sense of resentment was more than made up for by having a clever and beautiful wife who loved him, three enchanting children, a wide circle of friends and a lifestyle most people would envy.

As a family, the Baileys were much admired: 'If they weren't so nice,' as one of the other mothers at school said, 'you'd hate them.'

But they all were so extremely nice.

ACKNOWLEDGEMENTS

Many thanks to the following publications for permission to reproduce articles and interviews: *The Daily Mail*, *The Times*, Linda Mindel Carvell at *Surrey Occasions Magazine*, *Woman & Home*, *The Independent* and *The Sunday Express*.